# a
# stir
# of
# bones

BOOKS BY
# nina kiriki hoffman

*A Stir of Bones*

*A Fistful of Sky*

*Past the Size of Dreaming*

*A Red Heart of Memories*

*The Silent Strength of Stones*

*The Thread That Binds the Bones*

*Child of an Ancient City* (with Tad Williams)

*Unmasking*

# a
# stir
# of
# bones

*nina kiriki hoffman*

**VIKING**

VIKING
Published by Penguin Group
Penguin Young Readers Group, 345 Hudson Street,
New York, New York 10014, U.S.A.
Penguin Books Ltd, 80 Strand, London WC2R 0RL, England
Penguin Books Australia Ltd, 250 Camberwell Road,
Camberwell, Victoria 3124, Australia
Penguin Books Canada Ltd, 10 Alcorn Avenue,
Toronto, Ontario, Canada M4V 3B2
Penguin Books (N.Z.) Ltd, 182-190 Wairau Road, Auckland 10, New Zealand

Published in 2003 by Viking,
a division of Penguin Young Readers Group

3 5 7 9 10 8 6 4
Copyright © Nina Kiriki Hoffman, 2003

LIBRARY OF CONGRESS CATALOGING-IN-PUBLICATION DATA
Hoffman, Nina Kiriki.
A stir of bones / by Nina Kiriki Hoffman.
p. cm.
Summary: After discovering the secrets that lie in an abandoned house,
fourteen-year-old Susan Backstrom, with the help of some new friends,
has the ability to make a safe, new life for herself.
ISBN 0-670-03551-3 (hardcover)
[1. Haunted houses—Fiction. 2. Ghosts—Fiction. 3. Family
problems—Fiction. 4. Wife abuse—Fiction.] I. Title.
PZ7.H67567St 2003    [Fic]—dc21    2003005029

Printed in U.S.A.
Set in Century Schoolbook
Book design Teresa Kietlinski

This one's for two of my first readers:
Nancy Washburn, one of my high school roommates,
who always asked for more;
and Roberta Jeanne Whaley (a.k.a. Bobbi Hawes),
next-door neighbor extraordinaire (R.I.P.),
who taught me to love Fred Astaire movies and
Dorothy L. Sayers mysteries, and instructed all the neighborhood children in the intricacies of poker.

It's also for my editor, Sharyn November,
who always asks for more, too.

Thanks, you guys!

# a
# stir
# of
# bones

# chapter one

SUSAN'S GAZE SLID past her mirror image as she headed into the locker room, arrested, returned. What was that on the inside of her right thigh, below the hem of her blue gym shorts, that plum-purple oblong the size of her hand?

A bruise.

All the seventh-, eighth-, and ninth-grade girls trooped in off the marshy Oregon hockey field, filling the gray and gold girls' locker room at Heron Country Day School with warmth and movement, chatter and scents: sweat, deodorant, wet tennis shoes, perfume.

Girls stowed hockey sticks in lockers and changed from their P.E. uniforms into their regular school clothes. In her uniform, with her heavy silver-blonde hair tied back, Susan thought maybe she looked like all the others, enmeshed in the same web of banter and gossip.

That feeling of belonging never lasted.

She sighed, sat down, and took off her sneakers.

The chatter swept over her head as she removed her white short-sleeved uniform shirt and blue shorts, buttoned herself into her crisp white long-sleeved shirt, and zipped her plaid knee-length skirt.

She remembered how the bruise happened: she had run into Pam's hockey stick as Pam raised it to strike the ball.

Pam, tall, strong, always a team captain, her long dark frizzy hair unbound now, had changed from a teammate into Other in khaki slacks, peasant blouse, and sweater. She paused near Susan. "Sue, I'm really sorry."

Susan dropped her hem; it covered the bruise. She smiled at Pam. "That's okay. It was an accident."

"Does it hurt much?"

"Not a bit," said Susan. She never felt pain. She took secret pride in that power. Burns, cuts, scrapes: she watched them blister and bleed with clinical detachment, as if they were happening to someone on television.

"I wish there was something I could do," Pam said.

"Don't worry about it. It was my fault." Susan folded creases into her uniform.

"Well . . . have a nice weekend." Pam touched Susan's shoulder and walked away, glanced back just before she went out the door.

Susan stored her uniform in her locker, put her sports socks in a plastic bag to take home for the laundry basket. She laid a hand on her sneakers. Life would be lovely if one could live it in sneakers. She was never allowed to wear them at home. Father considered them unfeminine. She sat down, pulled on white knee socks, slid into shiny brown loafers.

By the time she had shrugged herself into her coat, the other girls had left. She looked toward the narrow strip of window that let in distant, clouded October sunlight, and listened to the faint sound of her breathing in the empty space of the locker room. With her eyes shut she sensed the space that opened out around her, not very high above her head, as she stood with her back to the lockers. The linoleum floor made the room feel different from carpeted space.

She leaned back, searching, as she often did, for a way to melt into the walls. This would be a strange but safe place to be part of a building. Girls talking, changing, and teasing for a small fraction of the day. No men except the janitor, who would come alone. So much safer than her house, though the house told her what was going on in it, and she knew where to hide.

She slung her blue cloth school bag over her shoulder, took her umbrella in one hand and her sea stone in the other, and walked toward the door with her eyes shut, listening to the echo of her footsteps between the banks of lockers. Someday she might go blind. She practiced for it.

Outside, the cool, damp coast air closed around her. A light fog had come in as afternoon leaned toward evening. Gym was final period. Everyone else had gone.

Today she was going to the public library to find books or magazines she could check out for her science project. This year she wanted to do a project on home computers. Nobody she knew had one, even though last year, 1981, almost a million and a half home computers had been sold to people in the United States. Susan had never actually seen a home computer except in advertisements. She was pretty sure things would change when everyone had a computer. She just needed to invent a hypothesis about how things would change, and then find somebody, more than one person if possible, who was using a computer, and test her hypothesis. If everybody had a computer, would people talk to each other anymore? Could a computer be your friend? If you had one, was it like opening a door into another world?

She couldn't test those sorts of things, but she could try to measure whether having a computer made a person change. If she could find someone who had a computer.

She had gotten special dispensation from Father to come home from school later than usual so she could research. He always supported her science projects, and had been thinking about getting a computer for his law office.

Instead of turning left at the end of the school driveway, she turned right, toward a part of Guthrie she rarely visited, the downtown part with stores, the movie theater, the DairyMaid, places other kids talked about between classes, places she had never been, or had only been once or twice.

Most days she went straight home to an empty house.

Susan's mother left the house every day she was well enough. Mother had meetings of the bridge club, the garden club, the book club, the watercolor club. On Mondays, she volunteered at the hospital. Every afternoon she stayed away from the house until just before Father came home; then she returned and heated up whatever Juanita, their housekeeper, had left for supper. Father liked the family to be together for supper.

Wednesdays, Susan went shopping at the supermarket with Juanita. Aside from that, Susan spent her afternoons home alone. She did homework. She read. She wasn't supposed to watch television after school. Father liked to decide what she could watch. He forbade nighttime dramas like *Dallas*, outlawed any viewing of the new TV station MTV, and encouraged her to watch PBS.

Sometimes Susan watched afternoon cartoons, even though they were on the forbidden list. She watched MTV, too. The culture there seemed utterly alien. She also spent hours lost in daydreams about all the things she might do if she were someone else.

Father called a couple of afternoons a week to make sure she was home—but never on the same days. She couldn't count on his not checking, so she always went home after school. If he ever checked and she wasn't there—

Today, with Father's permission, a little adventure. Maybe her quest was futile. Guthrie's public library didn't have many books. Home computers were too new for the library to have books on them, but she didn't care. She'd given herself a gift of time.

The public library was in a small two-story building. It was one place downtown that Susan had been to a lot. Whenever she had a weekend paper for class, her father would drop her off at the library on Saturday and pick her up, or she walked there and back. Father liked it better if he took her, though. He always wanted to know where she was and what she was doing.

Mrs. Garrison sat behind the front desk by the door, looming even though she was short, her hair in tight red curls, her glasses thick, with black frames. Susan had never seen her smile.

"What are you looking for today, missy?" she asked.

Susan smiled, pretended she was Mother, who always behaved like a princess in public. "Do you have any books about computers?"

"Not a blessed one." Mrs. Garrison pursed her lips. "Check the magazines, though. They write more about those infernal machines all the time."

Susan went to the periodicals section, where the most recent issues of magazines were kept. The library had no storage facilities except a shed, where older magazines went to wait for the library's annual sale. She grabbed recent issues of *Time* and *Newsweek* and took them upstairs to the nonfiction section, which had tables by the windows between tall, heavy bookcases. Susan had a favorite table, the one farthest from the stairs. From there she could look out at the ocean, imagine her way to the beach.

She got her three-ring binder and a Bic out of her

school bag and set up at her table. With lined paper in front of her and pen in hand, she opened the first magazine to the table of contents.

Below, the ocean was gray under a gray sky, and stretched away forever.

Happiness hummed inside her.

She had dropped down into study mind when she was roused half an hour later by the sound of people scraping chairs across linoleum, settling at the table just the other side of the shelves from her.

"We can't do it here," said a gruff girl's voice. "Can't count on being private."

"We have to find a better place," said a boy's voice. "Somewhere no one else will go. At home my little sister snoops all the time."

"Yeah, and my mom's home all afternoon," said the girl.

"I had a great idea during last period," said another boy.

Susan straightened, set her pen down silently. The first two voices she had never heard before, but the third she recognized: Julio, the son of Juanita, the housekeeper. Julio and Juanita were the only real friends Susan had.

She and Julio were both in seventh grade, but Julio went to the public middle school in downtown Guthrie. They had played with each other when Julio's mother first started housekeeping for Susan's family, nine years before. These days they rarely spoke.

"I mean, it's perfect. The haunted house," Julio murmured. "When's the last time you heard of anybody going there? Too many scary stories about it."

The haunted house! Susan had heard stories about it, too, girls muttering tales to scare each other when rain trapped them in study hall during recess. The haunted house was halfway between her house and Heron, at the end of an overgrown side street where no one ever went.

She pressed her hand to her chest. She couldn't feel her heartbeat. She lived in a haunted house, but no one else knew it. What would it be like to go to a house everyone knew was haunted?

"Wow," said the other boy. "That *is* a great idea. Maybe there's already—"

"Yeah, there's stories. Remember the one Trudie told in comp class?" asked the girl.

"Trudie," said the first boy.

"She's a world-class liar," Julio said, an edge to his voice. Susan had never heard him say anything mean about anyone before.

"Sure," said the girl impatiently. "We know that. We found out the hard way. She sounds so good, though. Everybody always believes her, even though nobody likes her. 'Cause she says stuff that sounds true, and sometimes it *is* true. She said she knew somebody who went in the haunted house to spend the night on a dare, and when he came out the next morning his hair was all white, and he died a week later. His heart gave out."

"Did she name names?" Julio asked.

"No."

"She can't name names, because it never actually happened," said Julio. "She's so full of it."

"But that's good," said the other boy. "If she tells everyone scary stories about it, people will stay away. *She'll* stay away."

"'Cause maybe there's a good reason to stay away," the girl said, her voice even lower than it had been.

"I vote we check it out," said Julio. "Walk up to the front porch, anyway. While it's still light. Tomorrow's Saturday. We could do it then."

"Right. Tomorrow, early. You're not chicken, are you, Dee?" asked the other boy. His tone was teasing.

"I'm not afraid of anything," said the girl.

Susan touched her fingertips to her wrist. She could never find her pulse. She gave up, shoved her notebook into her school bag and dropped the pen in after it, curled her hand around her sea stone, pushed back her chair with a scraping noise, and stood.

The others quieted. Susan's legs shook. How odd. She peeked around the end of the bookcase. Julio and a strange boy and girl stared her direction.

"Oh," said Julio. "Susan." He wore a black sweatshirt. His brown sugar face paused somewhere between expressions, his black eyes intent.

They hardly spoke anymore. But this was the first time in her memory that he wasn't happy to see her. Then again, she was interrupting their private meeting.

If she'd just stayed still, they would never have known she was there.

"We forgot to check for spies. I can't believe we forgot to check!" said the girl, her voice ferocious. She looked wiry and short, with thick untidy brown braids down her back and shaggy bangs over her forehead. Dark brows frowned above her tea brown eyes. Her face was square-jawed. She wore a bright purple rain slicker with red trim.

The other boy had curly light-brown hair. He had an angular jaw and hazel eyes, and he wore jeans and an off-white fisherman's sweater. He frowned at Susan.

"Hi," she said, trying her princess smile.

Julio sat up. "Hi, Susan. These are my friends, Edmund and Deirdre. Guys, my friend Susan."

"She's your friend?" Deirdre asked.

"Sure."

"From where? She doesn't go to Guthrie Middle School."

"My mom works for her mom."

"So how's that—" the girl began.

The other boy stood up and held out a hand. "Hi, Susan."

"Pleased to meet you." Susan shook his hand. He had long fingers, and his palm was dry, his grip firm.

He smiled at her, held her right hand with his right, jiggled his left hand, and snapped his fingers. A red chicken-feather flower appeared in his left hand. He let go of her and offered her the flower.

"Stop that, Edmund! Don't waste magic on her! We're *not* pleased to meet *you*," said the girl. "Were you eavesdropping on us?"

"Not on purpose." She took the flower, touched it to her face, stared wonderingly at Edmund. No boy had ever given her a flower before. Besides, he had made it appear from nowhere. Did it mean something special?

The girl's hands tightened into fists on the tabletop. "Yeah. I can't believe what idiots we were! How dumb were we not to check?"

"It's all right," Julio said. "Susan doesn't gossip."

"I won't tell anyone," Susan said. She swallowed, lowered the flower to her side. "But I want to go with you."

# chapter two

ON SATURDAY MORNING, Susan opened her eyes and stared up at the strawberry pink canopy sprinkled with tiny bouquets of roses. She reached over and turned off the alarm clock chiming on the white-and-gold nightstand. After blinking away dreams, she sat up and fished her sea stone from under her pillows, then lifted a ruffled pink curtain to peer at the morning sky. It was overcast but not spitting.

She let the curtain drop and paused in the midst of pink sheets and pillows, pink quilts and spread, and looked at her sea stone.

When wet it was nearly black, but dry it faded to pale blue-gray. The edge of a spiraled fossil of a shell showed white in the dark matrix. Every morning, feeling as though she woke in a strawberry-and-marshmallow ice-cream sundae, Susan stroked her stone and remembered the day she had found it.

Even though Guthrie lay along the sea, Susan wasn't allowed to spend much time on the beach. Father considered the sand too messy. But one summer when

Susan was eight, Aunt Caroline and Uncle Henry visited, and Aunt Caroline had spirited Susan down to the beach. Susan had dipped bare toes into the icy water, run from sneaker waves, and watched people fly long-tailed kites. She had collected agates and colored rocks, treasures of texture and shape, but at the end of the day, she had cast all of them except this one back into the ocean, knowing she would never be allowed to keep such formless, worthless things.

This one sea stone, which fit into her hand so well, she knew she could keep with her always; it, memories, and the sunburn on her nose were all she had taken home that day. Five years later, the memories and the stone still comforted her and kept her as steady as she could manage. The delicate spiral locked in stone had lasted millions of years. Things could survive a lot of sand grinding and seagoing.

Deirdre was a grinder.

Maybe Susan had some sand in her, too. She couldn't believe she had broken in on a private conversation between people she didn't even know and demanded that they let her join them. She had never done anything like that before.

She wasn't sure how long this chance would last. It amazed her that she had found it and taken it. Since she was working on a school project, she even had the opportunity to be out of the house without getting pun-ished for it.

Julio was all right with her joining them, and

Edmund seemed not to mind, though he had the biggest secret, Susan suspected, the thing the others wanted to help him protect.

But Deirdre resented everything about Susan.

Maybe that wouldn't change. Maybe this day was the only special one she'd have.

She could savor a good memory forever.

Today she would have an adventure.

Only, what should she wear? She set the stone on her dresser and went to the closet.

Father loved the picture she made, blonde hair, blue eyes, the roses in her cheeks, as she wore crisp linen blouses, pleated skirts, smart little sweater vests, a navy blazer with the Heron School crest over the left breast, pointed-toed shoes.

She also had gowns for Father's social events, where her purpose was to be visible and silent: the eyelet-embroidered white lawn summer dress with lace inserts, a delicate antique that had belonged to Father's grandmother and fit Susan eerily well, though the fabric was so old and fragile she was scared to brush against anything when she wore it, almost scared to breathe for fear of splitting something; the smart, short black velvet dress, evening wear, that made her look grown up; the pink floral print on black crepe for afternoons, gallery openings or teas.

She didn't have a single outfit suitable for breaking into a haunted house.

She went to the dresser and touched her sea stone

again. It was rough and hard; it felt like a key that unlocked her image and let the real person out.

What if she got dirty?

Deirdre probably never gave dirt a moment's thought.

But for Susan—if Father thought—if Father knew. . . . She tried not to think about the times he had been angry with her, the days Mother didn't leave the house.

Susan decided to wear one of her standard school outfits: blouse, jacket, pleated skirt, knee socks, and loafers. She packed a change of clothes in her school bag. If the first got dirty, she could change before she came home. Father need not know. Only Juanita saw the dirty laundry.

She packed socks and underwear, too, then smiled and added a toothbrush. As if she could run away. As if she could stay away.

She packed her notebook and pencils to have an excuse to be gone all day. Sea stone in hand, she went to her bedroom door and listened with her eyes closed. A humming awareness opened up as she checked in with the house. No movement from Mother's room, two closets away from hers; no movement from Father's room, across the stairwell from hers. She couldn't sense any dish noises from the kitchen, just below her room, and she hadn't heard the stairs' characteristic creaks since she woke up. Good. Perhaps Father was sleeping in. He did that some Saturdays, and Mother did, too, if left alone.

She knew where the stairs creaked, and avoided the spots on her way down. She slipped into the kitchen for a second, grabbed an apple and two slices of bread, and tucked them into her pack. She had just fetched her raincoat from the closet under the stairs when a voice said, "And just where are you going, young lady?"

She turned. Father stood in the door to his study. He was tall and blond, with muscular shoulders. She kept her gaze on the white monogram on his blue velvet bathrobe. She almost never looked him in the eye.

"Down to the library," she said. "More research for my science project."

"That's my girl." He placed his hand on her head. She tightened her fist around the sea stone and stopped herself from flinching. "Be back in time for lunch."

"Oh, Father, I don't know. I'm taking my notebook. I might get some of my writing done in the library. I need an investigation plan, you know, and I'm still reading through current events in magazines to find my main question."

His hand lingered on her head. Then he stroked her hair. "Be back for supper, then," he said, this time in his you-can't-refuse voice.

"Yes, Father." She went slowly down the front steps, feeling his gaze on her like a hand on the back of her neck. Then she heard the door close, and she ran into the cool mist, a helium lightness filling her.

"Susan?" Julio called from her left. He came down

the bank, his high-tops pattering on the pavement.

"Yes," she said. "I can't stop now." She ran down the damp road, her leather shoes slippery on the asphalt, but she ran too fast to fall, and Julio kept up with her. The road rounded a curve and rose again, slowing her a little, but she laughed, her school bag banging her side, and the sea stone a good solid weight in her hand. She had freed a whole day for herself. She glanced at her watch, a tiny gold wafer with a black face and no numbers, only a diamond where the twelve should be, and thought about the arc the hour hand would make around it before she had to be home again. From eight all the way to five. Most of a day, all of the daylight. Amazing.

"Where are we going, anyway?" she asked at last.

"Lee Street," said Julio.

Susan breathed deeply. The air tasted and smelled like the sea. As they came down the hill past other wealthy and isolated houses, she heard the unceasing hush of distant waves on a distant beach. They descended to where houses clustered closer together and streets crossed each other more often.

On Lee Street, Julio led her around the back of a large green house surrounded by shaggy lawn. He knocked on the kitchen door. A woman in a turquoise jogging outfit with white sleeves pushed a brown forelock out of her eyes and greeted them. "Hi. I'm Edmund's mother. You must be Susan. You can call me Beverly." She shook hands with Susan vigorously, and let them into a sprawling kitchen. Deirdre and a little girl were arguing about who got a piece of toast. Edmund rose from a chair beside a man who lowered his newspaper long enough to smile at them.

Deirdre stood up, conceding the toast to the little girl. She glared at Susan, then sighed.

"You going somewhere?" said the little girl. "Can I come too?"

Edmund groaned and said, "No, Abby, no, Abby, no," as if it were a well-worn chant.

"Go on, get out of here," said Beverly, shooing them away. "And don't you forget about that lawn, Edmund. This is the third week you promised."

"I won't." He snatched a backpack from a pile of things on one of the counters.

Deirdre grabbed a red plastic flashlight off the table and followed the rest of them outside.

Their destination was only a couple of blocks from Edmund's house, but the street they followed to get there grew increasingly potholed, its borders more jungly every foot of the way. Susan had seen blackberry bushes everywhere in town; they sprang up on disturbed sites and, if left alone, ran riot. But these, and the stunted shore pines that hunched inland under the constant sea wind, looked denser and darker than those she had seen before.

At the end of the street stood a picket fence, some of its pickets missing, some crooked, the fence itself weathered, all the paint worn off to leave silvery wood behind.

It sagged outward, fencing a yard full of blackberry castles, canes reaching up, intertwining, looping over higher than head height. A battered gate hung about six inches open. Beyond it, a narrow trail twisted between the brambles.

Above the thorny bushes, a peaky, shingled roof of many parts thrust up against the mist. At one end was a square tower. Dark gaps like missing teeth broke the lines of mossy fish-scale shingles.

"Wow," said Deirdre. "Pretty creepy."

Edmund led them to the fence. He glanced at the others. "I've come this far a thousand times," he said, "but I've never gone inside the gate." He stared toward what they could see of the house, leaned forward.

"We could go back to the library," Julio said.

"I can't do my—you couldn't practice—we couldn't— And anyway, this is one place we can be pretty sure she won't follow us," Edmund muttered. He gripped one of the fence pickets. "Please. Let's go in."

Susan laid a hand on the worn wood of the fence. What lay under its surface? What memories had it collected? Did it know things the way her house did, some of the walls soured with tears, puffy with swallowed screams, slippery with secrets? She clutched the sea stone tight.

Dew hung heavy on the five-fingered tooth-edged leaves of the blackberry vines, but the fence didn't feel wet. It felt almost silky, the no-temperature of dry wood to the touch—and then, faint and far away, she felt a hum. A warmth.

"Do we just go up to the front door?" she asked.

"I guess first we see if we can get past the gate," said Edmund.

He touched the latch, tugged at it. The gate creaked open, its hinges thawing with screeches. Showers of orange rust flaked off, flavoring the air with iron.

Beer bottles gleamed under the bushes nearest the gate, and plastic bags, white, beige, yellow, had snagged on some of the brambles. Edmund took the first step onto the narrow footpath beyond the gate. It was a strange path, grassy, untraveled. There were no footprints on it. Most of the litter looked as if it had been tossed from the street over the fence.

Susan followed Edmund, and Julio and Deirdre followed her.

The path led past walls of stacked brambles. They had to go sideways for some of it, and even then Deirdre left a few hairs on one cane; Edmund lost a tuft of sweater wool on another.

About twenty-five feet in, they approached a small clearing in front of the house. Broken steps led up to a chest-high front porch. The house looked dark and decrepit and mysterious. It had an odd tower on the right corner, round on the bottom story and rectangular upstairs. Its sides were covered with alternating strips of round, oval, and rectangular shingles. Some had fallen off, leaving gaps. Not much paint remained, hardly a hint of the house's original color—maybe something dark.

"That porch doesn't look safe. Let's go around back,

see what we find," Deirdre muttered. "It's more hidden from the street."

Another path took them around the side of the house.

The back porch sagged in the middle, and some of its planks had fallen through. But it was closer to the ground than the front porch and, as Deirdre had said, less visible; the back of the house faced onto a thicket of alder trees on the edge of a little ravine.

Edmund tested each step before he put his weight on it. Deirdre passed him on the porch and rattled the rusty doorknob, but the back door held. "I guess that's a good sign," she said. "Maybe nobody else goes inside. I brought a bunch of keys—all I could find." She fished a large key ring out of her coat pocket. "I brought my Swiss Army knife too. It has a screwdriver on it in case everything else fails."

She tried keys in the lock. Edmund investigated the contents of his backpack. Julio stood back, hands in his pockets, and watched Deirdre work.

Susan passed the others and went to a window. She wiped away mist and dust and peered inside. An old pump, its handle poised at the top of its arch, stood above a tublike sink. A squat stove sat on flagstones against a side wall. The kitchen. She put her sea stone in her school bag and laid both hands flat against the house's shingled wall.

The wall felt warm, even in the wet, heavy morning. She moved closer, leaned her cheek against the wall, and closed her eyes. She could almost hear the house's slow breath. It sounded like sleep. And then—it almost seemed to come awake, to sense *her*; something fluttered its slow pulse—

"Got it," said Deirdre, her voice rich with triumph. Susan sensed the door opening. The house groaned.

Susan took a deep breath and opened her eyes. She heard the others' steps as they entered the house. Reluctantly, she let go of the wall and followed.

The door opened into a short hall. One door opened into a dark room, and another led into the kitchen. The others went toward light and the kitchen.

"Look at it," said Deirdre from the kitchen. "It's not even very dusty." They moved on through the kitchen and out another door beyond Susan's sight. She patted the back door and followed the hall into the kitchen.

She touched the stove's black surface. Flakes of paint dropped off. She knelt beside the stove, upset that she had disturbed whatever order existed, and pressed her hand over the flakes, hoping they would stick to her palm so she could brush them off outside. She glanced toward the doorway the others had gone through. They stood at the far end of the room beyond, talking. A moment later, they turned a corner, out of her sight.

She fished the sea stone out of her school bag, stared from it to the paint flakes. She smelled the rust in the stove, and felt the air moving in the house, fresh air invading stale. The light that came in the kitchen windows filtered through a layer of grime; soft gray sunlight lay across the dusty old counters and the wood floor. She turned back to the stove. ACME BOOMER, it said on the oven door, surrounded by a wealth of curlicues. She set the stone on one of the burner covers on top, laid her hand on the cool rusty steel.

Suddenly the atmosphere shifted.

A moan started in the heart of the house. Low at first, it rose in pitch and volume, filled with all the pain in the world.

It sounded like her mother.

Susan touched her face, dipped fingertips in tears. She wondered if the moan came from her.

"God," said Deirdre. "What is it?" Her voice was terrified. "*Who* is it?"

With a thud of running footsteps, Deirdre and Julio burst through the kitchen, ran past Susan, down the hall, and out the back door.

Susan rose. Their panic infected her. She ran from the house, away from the tearing brambles, out the gate after the others until she had to gasp for breath. They slowed and she caught up to them half a block down the street.

"Wait," said Deirdre between gasps. "Where's Edmund?"

They stood, panting, and looked up the street. The mist had burned away, but nowhere in the vista of cloudy sky and dew-burnished trees, brambles, and street was there a sign of Edmund.

"We have to go back," said Julio.

# chapter three

SUSAN HUGGED HERSELF. She had left her school bag inside, and her sea stone. She remembered the welcoming warmth she had felt from the house; she started back toward it. The others followed her. "Where did you lose Edmund?" she asked.

"What do you mean, lose him?" Deirdre cried.

Julio said at the same time, "He was halfway up the stairs when the noise started. I thought he was right behind us when we ran."

"Maybe he tripped," Susan said.

Deirdre pushed past her. "He should have come out by now." She scanned the street. An old man plucked a newspaper from his wet lawn and waved to them. Susan waved back. "He should have," Deirdre whispered.

She was scared, Susan realized. Deirdre was scared. Susan lowered her head to let her hair fall around her face. She smiled. She walked faster, leading the way to the back porch.

"Can't you be sneakier?" Deirdre whispered furiously, pulling on Susan's sleeve. Susan glanced back. The man had gone inside, and there was no one else on the street except several cats. Susan pulled her sleeve free and went on around the house.

The back door stood open. Susan crossed the porch, then stopped, her hand on the doorjamb, and listened. She heard voices, arguing. She stepped inside. "Edmund? Edmund, are you all right?"

"I'm fine," he called.

Julio ran through the kitchen toward the front of the house with Deirdre on his heels. Susan paused long enough to pick up her school bag and her stone, then followed.

"Someone else had our idea first," Edmund said as Susan crossed the dining room to where the others stood at the base of the stairs.

Wide windows let in dusty sun. Cobwebs dropped lines from the shadowy ceiling.

For an instant, Susan thought she saw a table and chairs to her left; they turned to shadows, then vanished.

The others stood in a wide hall that opened out of the dining room. Stairs went up to a large landing, then turned and ascended into darkness. Edmund's curly hair had straightened into dripping strings, and his sweater was wet.

"He moved in before we could. That's who did the moaning, the guy who was here first," said Edmund. He swiped his wet hair out of his eyes.

"Where is he?"

"He hid when he heard Susan's voice just now. When we ran, I tripped and hit my head coming down the stairs, and he threw water on me to wake me up. He apologized. He didn't mean to hurt anyone, just wanted to scare us." Edmund glanced around, then narrowed his eyes. "Nathan?" he called. "These are my friends."

The silence thickened as they waited. Deirdre licked her lips. Julio stared up into the darkness.

"Nathan?"

Susan leaned against the wall. It was warm on her back. The house was breathing: not the slow breaths of a sleeper, but the quick ones of something awake and interested.

Julio hunched his shoulders and glanced around, as if he sensed a hidden watcher.

Deirdre scuffed her feet.

"Nathan, stop playing games and come out." Edmund didn't sound very sure of himself.

The moan began again. It came from beneath their feet, then from the front of the house, then from the ceiling. Deirdre grabbed Julio's arm.

"Some sound system, huh?" said Edmund.

Susan rubbed her eyes.

"Nathan, stop that right now," Edmund said in a teacher tone of voice. Frowning, he looked through doorways—into the small room off the dining room, into the living room across the hall, and toward the front door. When he didn't spot anyone or anything, he started up the stairs.

The house shook. Dust puffed up from cracks in the wood floor, and the banister wobbled in Edmund's hand. The moans crescendoed, then faded to an unnerving near-sob.

Something honeydew-sized and pale emerged from the upstairs darkness, rolled and clattered down the stairs. It came to rest on the hall floor. A skull. They had only a moment to recognize it before it rolled again, toward Julio and Deirdre. Deirdre screamed and clung to Julio, who clung back.

Susan laughed. A plastic skull. How silly. She'd spent time studying bone reproductions in science class, curious about how bodies were put together, what lodged under the skin. She dropped her sea stone into her skirt pocket, walked over, and picked up the skull.

It was not plastic; it was light and hard and dry, the cranium smooth and the facial bones rough. The jawbone came loose in her hand. She touched the enameled teeth, then ran her tongue over her own teeth. A strange, unfamiliar sadness overwhelmed her. She hugged the skull to her stomach and closed her eyes. Heat under her eyelids. A hot tear escaped to cool on her cheek.

The moaning had stopped, and so had the shaking. The house held its breath. Susan opened her eyes and turned to the others. They stared at her. "It's real," she said, her throat tight. She held out the skull.

They stared, Deirdre open-mouthed.

Susan stroked the skull, locked into an empathy with something unknown, unseen.

"Stop that," said a new voice.

He stood on the landing. He was slender, about the same age as they were, with blue eyes, black hair long enough to brush his shirt collar, and the face of a graveyard angel. His round shirt collar rose high on his neck; suspenders made black stripes against his white shirt. Dark knickers buckled under the knees. He wore black knee stockings and ankle-high black shoes.

He walked down the stairs past Edmund and came to her. "Stop it." He held out his hands for the skull.

Susan hugged it again, and he closed his eyes. His smile flickered, then disappeared. He said, "No. I'm sorry. You can't have it; it's mine."

Susan's sadness vanished, leaving heady euphoria. "But you're mistreating it. You threw it down the stairs. That's the same as throwing it away, and finders keepers."

"Now, look." He paused, his face alive with smile. "What would you do with it, anyway?"

She fitted the jawbone back in place, nesting the hinges up in the cavities behind the flaring arches of the cheekbones. "I'll keep it someplace safe." But where in her house was safe? Her father often went through her things, and Juanita did, too, by necessity. The only place she could have secrets was in her head. "Well, I'll keep it here, I guess." She studied the skull, glanced at him. "May I keep it here?"

He looked from the others to her. "Would you want to visit it?"

She peered at the skull, then closed her eyes a moment, listening to the house. It felt so different from her father's house, much more alive, and somehow comfortable. "Yes."

"This house is supposed to be haunted. I can't have people coming here all the time. It would destroy my reputation."

"We could help you haunt," said Susan.

"Not that you need it," Deirdre muttered.

"I can't have you coming here," said the boy.

"I guess I'll have to take it home, then," Susan said. "I'll find someplace to hide it." Maybe the garden shed out back. No, the gardener used that. What about her locker at school? It would be weird if someone broke in and discovered the skull. There had to be a good place at home where her father wouldn't look. Well, maybe not. He looked everywhere, saw everything. Out in the yard maybe?

She cradled the skull against one hip and reached into her pocket for her sea stone. As her hand closed around it, she remembered the day she had found it. She thought, then turned back. "Look." She held out her sea stone, with the white fossil showing. "I'll give you this."

He held his hands up, open. "You don't understand. It's my skull. You can't take it."

"This is my sea stone." The joy left her as swiftly as it had come.

"Yes. I understand it's precious. But—"

"How did you make the house shake?" Deirdre asked. Before the boy turned to face her, she made shooing motions at Susan. "Is there some kind of motor in it?"

"It's difficult to explain," the boy said.

Susan tiptoed toward the kitchen, hardly able to believe Deirdre was helping her.

"It doesn't exactly work according to the laws of physical science," continued the boy's voice.

Susan didn't understand why she wanted the skull so much. It was narrow and had very beautiful teeth. It was small, almost delicate, elegant in its curves and arches. Holding it gave her a strange sense that she touched a past, a life, that inside the dome of it was a whole world.

Deirdre kept prompting the boy in the front hall.

Susan stopped in the kitchen and set her sea stone on the stove. She headed for the back door, still wide open.

She stepped to the doorsill, but couldn't go farther. It was as though an invisible wall prevented the skull from crossing the threshold. She set the skull down and went outside. From the porch, she reached for the skull, but it resisted.

She felt as though she were playing tug-of-war with the house.

She went back inside.

She tried pushing the skull out the door. It bumped into an invisible barrier and stopped on the threshold.

At last Susan sighed and went into the kitchen, where she sat beside the stove with the skull in her lap. She studied it, ran her thumb along the brow ridges.

"Does that make it easier for you to understand?" the boy asked from the dining room doorway.

"It belongs here." She sighed. "Don't throw it around anymore, though."

"I won't make that mistake again."

"All right." She set the skull on her knee. "I probably couldn't visit very often, anyway."

"Why not?"

"Her father keeps track of her time." Julio followed the boy into the kitchen. "How'd you get this morning off, Susan?"

"I told him I was going to the library to work on my science project. I should head down there and get some research done. He checks all my schoolwork."

"Go tell your friends they can't go upstairs," the boy said to Julio.

"How did you know?" Julio grinned.

"House tells me everything. If they get to the first landing, they'll be shaken right off the stairs. We regret Edmund's fall earlier, but we'll do it again if we have to."

Julio lost his smile and went back into the dining room. The boy sat down facing Susan. "I'm Nathan," he said. "You're—Susan?"

"Yes," she said, and held out her hand.

He bit his lip, glanced at the ceiling, nodded once, and put his hand in hers. It was very cold and slender.

"You're freezing," she whispered, and clasped his hand in both of hers. It did not take warmth. She reached up to feel his forehead. It was as cold as the sea. "Oh, Nathan, we better get you to a doctor! You're sick!" She leaned forward to put her arms around him, trying to hug warmth into him.

She closed her eyes and stroked his back, marveling at herself for touching another human being, and a boy at that.

The skull fell off her knee. Suddenly she embraced empty air.

"Susan." Deirdre tugged Susan's hand. "We've got to get out of here. It isn't safe."

Edmund took her other hand and hoisted her up.

"But where did he go?" she asked.

"What?" asked Deirdre. "The house shakes, but there's no machine doing it, I don't think. We should find some other place to hide out. Let's go."

"But Nathan—"

"Take the skull." Deirdre nodded toward the skull on the floor.

"It won't leave the house." Susan glanced around the kitchen. Only Julio, Edmund, and Deirdre were present. "Nathan's sick. He shouldn't be left alone."

"Nathan," yelled Julio. "We're leaving. You want us to take you to a doctor?"

"Too late for that," said Nathan's voice, but it didn't come from any single direction.

"Oh, stop that spooky stuff and come here," Susan

said. "You can't scare us anymore. You need help. Let us help you."

Edmund shook his head, his lips tight.

"You can't help me." Nathan came out of the hall that led to the back door. "No one can."

"Don't say that," said Susan. He sounded like she usually felt. She moved through her days on a set track, and whenever she stepped off the track, horrible things happened. And yet, here she was, with three other people, two of whom she had only met yesterday, and maybe nothing awful would come of it. Maybe there was a way to escape the trap of routine. "We could be friends. We could help you. We could get you a doctor."

"I don't think I'm allowed friends," he said, "and a doctor wouldn't help."

"Who tells you what you're allowed to do?"

"It's complicated," he said.

"It doesn't exactly work according to the laws of physical science," said Edmund. Nathan looked at him. Edmund crossed his arms and hunched his shoulders.

"That's right," said Nathan. He shoved his hands into his pockets and scowled at the floor. "I haven't done anything right since you grabbed the skull. It's been one not-allowed thing after another." He glanced at Susan. "I don't know how to fix this; I might as well try the truth."

He looked up at the ceiling for a long moment, then closed his eyes and sighed. "I'm not sick, Susan. I'm dead."

# chapter four

"NO," SAID DEIRDRE, shaking her head. She backed away until she hit the kitchen counter.

Edmund stepped closer to Susan and put a steadying hand on her shoulder.

"Then it *is* your house," said Susan. "You ought to be able to invite any guests you like."

Nathan laughed. Behind him, the back door slammed shut.

"Didn't you hear what he said?" Julio asked Susan. "Either he's dead or crazy. This is no time for Miss Manners."

"He's dead," said Edmund.

"How can you talk about it? How can you be calm?" Deirdre cried. She reached over the counter and tugged at the window, tried to force it open. "I'm going to scream. I really do feel like it." She turned and faced the boy. "Let us out, okay? Please?"

He stepped aside, leaving the hallway clear, and she ran past, rattled the back doorknob. "It won't open," she said, her voice rising. "Open it. Please."

"But I didn't close it. I can't open it. House has a mind of its own," said Nathan, "and I don't know what it's thinking right now. This isn't the way things are supposed to go."

"So what's supposed to happen?" Julio asked. His voice shook. "Are we all supposed to die?"

"No. You run away screaming, and tell everyone how scary it is here."

"But we can't." Deirdre jerked the doorknob.

Susan slipped away from Edmund and went to the kitchen wall. She placed her hands flat on it. The house was breathing more rapidly.

She leaned against the wall, wondering at its warmth. It felt welcoming. She sensed a laugh inside it. She pressed her cheek against it, closed her eyes, breathed deeply in time with the house.

The house was alive, and the boy wasn't.

She lived within narrow bounds, trapped and constrained, and yet, within those boundaries, she had a certain freedom. She could touch trees, smell flowers, breathe sea air, feel rain against her skin. She could watch the world going by past a car window; she could run around on a marshy field with a bunch of other girls, swinging hockey sticks, get glorious bruises and hide them; she could talk to people, even if she didn't know how yet.

She thought of the boy, bound inside the house, scaring people away when they ventured closer. Things weren't supposed to go this way. And yet . . . she remembered his cheek on her shoulder.

"How many years have you been doing this, Nathan?" she asked.

"Sixty-three."

"Maybe it's time for things to change," she said.

She licked her lip and looked at the others. Edmund had his arms crossed. Julio watched her with his eyebrows up. Deirdre had come back into the kitchen. She let out a big breath. "Yeah," Deirdre said, "something's got to change. We can't hang around here for the next sixty-three years. The house has to let us out."

Susan stepped away from the wall and picked up the skull. "Maybe the house wants us to stay, or at least visit. Maybe the house disagrees with Nathan."

"We're talking about a house that throws people off staircases, Susan," said Julio.

"That was before it knew us."

"You expect things to be different now?" asked Deirdre. "You think it—it *knows* us?"

"We don't even know each other," Susan said. She gave a huge sigh. "Maybe it *wants* to know us." She looked at Nathan. She held out the skull. The air in the room tightened, as if the house waited, like a stalking cat watching several mice. Susan felt there were words she could say that would set something loose, but she wasn't sure which ones.

Edmund smiled. He stepped forward and laid his hand on the skull. "How about this? All for one and one for all."

Susan listened to the silence in the house. It still

waited. She looked at Julio and Deirdre, and after a moment, they stepped forward. Julio put his hand on top of Edmund's, and Deirdre laid her hand on Julio's hand.

The air was still tense.

Susan looked at Nathan. She could see through him; he was wavery, very pale and uncertain. His eyes were wide, the ice-blue irises nearly swallowed by the dark pupils. He took a hesitant step forward. Susan felt a strange tingling sadness again. She watched him walk to them, and felt each step as though it were hers. She had taken that walk— yesterday afternoon, this morning—and arrived here, too. Nobody said it would work; nobody said they wouldn't get in terrible trouble for walking out of the way they had existed for years.

He placed his hand on Deirdre's. Deirdre shivered. Susan laid her free hand on Nathan's; his felt chill but solid.

She looked up. They were watching her. "All right," she said. "Ready?"

It would be so easy for this to seem too stupid to do. They nodded.

"All for one and one for all," they said.

The house gave a contented sigh. The back door groaned open.

# chapter five

SUSAN WALKED UP the stairs to the first landing. "All right." She smiled down at the others. From the landing she could see a little light from upstairs, where Nathan waited.

She held Nathan's skull in both hands. She knew she would find a hiding place for it.

Edmund climbed the stairs to join her. Deirdre watched with narrowed eyes, but the stairs remained calm and did not throw him off. So she steamed up after him, with Julio in her wake.

Susan went up the next set of stairs and stopped beside Nathan to glance around. There were a number of corners and doors, but to the left, the space opened up. She walked over and found herself between two window seats in the square upstairs section of the tower room. The windows in the three walls had clear central panes with narrow borders of stained glass cut in rectangles. She felt as though she were in the house's lookout; she had a good view across the brambles to Lee Street.

"I've always wondered what it was like up here,"

Edmund said from behind her. "This is great!" He patted a sun-faded seat cushion. "But why isn't there more dust?"

"House accumulates some dust and cobwebs downstairs," said Nathan. "Nobody comes upstairs, so it doesn't bother up here." He stood in front of one of the doors.

Susan held up the skull. "Where's the rest of you?"

"I'm the only ghost here," he said.

"The rest of the skeleton."

He gave her a measuring glance. "Behind a secret panel. That part got out. I don't know—House does it. I can't open the doors, just go through them."

"Oh," said Julio. "Huh." He reached for the handle of the door Nathan stood beside, and pulled the door open. Beyond was a fully furnished bedroom. They went inside.

Feathery green leaves curled amid scatters of dull flowers on the carpet. The bed had head- and footboards of dark wood. To their left stood a dresser with a large round mirror on a stand above it, and a tall wardrobe. To the right, there was a roll-topped desk and a long bookcase.

Susan went to sit on the bed.

"All this furniture," said Deirdre. "How come they took all the stuff downstairs and left this?"

"I don't know," said Nathan. "That part isn't clear to me. I didn't wake up directly after I died. When I first haunted, I sleepwalked through it. I didn't know what I was doing or who was around. House helped me figure it out later.

"Some ghosts are just leftover emotions. They do the same thing every time in the same place. I started out as one of those, and then something woke me up. When I woke up, the downstairs had been stripped, my mother's room was like this, and some distant cousins had moved in." He rubbed his eyes. "I scared them. The little girls. That was cruel, but they put them in the room where I—" He frowned, shook his head. "I manifested there for a couple years before they moved, though."

"Nathan, are the rumors true? Did you kill yourself?" Julio asked.

Nathan raised fingers to the button at his throat, undid it, and pulled his collar loose, revealing dark rope burns around his neck.

Deirdre closed her eyes. "Why?"

He rebuttoned his shirt. "It has been such a long time. Those thoughts had a strong hold on me, but they've had time to fade now."

"You remember," Susan said, "when you moan. I bet you remember."

"I remember there was a war in Europe, the biggest war the world had ever seen. We sent people over there to win the war, and pieces of people came back. My father volunteered as a medic. He always expected to die young, because everyone in our family did. He wasn't in combat, but he was badly wounded. A nurse wrote to us from a hospital in England when I was thirteen, and Mother left me here to go to him. Her ship went down on the way over. The post brought notices of her death and my father's just a few days apart." He sat on the floor and stared at his hands, which lay, half-curled, in his lap.

"I managed to survive for a year on my own here. Some of my friends helped me. I sold off bits and pieces of things from the house.

"There was a horrible influenza epidemic in 1918. People died everywhere, and lay unburied in the streets. I hadn't eaten in a couple of days—ran out of money and odd jobs, and the Halley store wouldn't extend my credit. One night I thought I had the influenza symptoms. I was alone in the house, and the enemy was here, inside me—" He flattened his hand on his chest. "So I made this decision."

After a moment, Deirdre said, "Do you want your bones buried in consecrated ground? Is that what you're waiting for?"

"I don't think so." He looked up at her. "It's not that simple. I'm not even sure it's a—a consummation devoutly to be wished. Look. You're here. Things just changed. I want to stay and see what happens next." He straightened. "Who are you people?"

"Deirdre Eberhard."

"Edmund Reynolds."

"Julio Rivera."

"Susan Backstrom."

"Nathaniel Blacksmith," Nathan said. "These are just names. Who are you?"

"Do you mean what do we want to do with our lives? When I was a little kid, I wanted to be a pirate," said Deirdre. She frowned. "Now I'm not sure what I want. I love animals. Maybe I'll be a vet. Or I could be a jewel thief, or maybe a spy. Julio's going to be a musician, and Edmund—that's a secret. I don't know about Susan. What are you going to be?" Deirdre asked her.

Susan's mind went blank.

"She'll be a homecoming queen, and then she'll get married," said Deirdre, after waiting a moment for Susan's reply.

"No!" Susan jumped to her feet, her hands tightening around the skull. "No! I won't! That's what my mother did!"

Julio stared at her, eyes wide.

"Hey, you can be the president of the United States if you want." Deirdre shrugged. "I think it helps if you have a plan, though. That's why I should figure out mine. Wait too long and you fall into something. I don't want to end up a housewife like my mom."

"I know what I plan," Susan said. Her voice came out quiet and intense. "I plan to leave home and never go back." Suddenly she heard her own breathing. It was fast and loud, and it had an echo. The house inhaled and exhaled with her. She realized she had just put into words something she had never even whispered to herself. She looked at the others. They were all watching her, and that, too, felt scary.

She stared down at the skull, then glanced at Nathan. "Where's the secret panel, Nathan?"

"In my room," he said.

"Show me. Please."

He drifted to the door. She opened it, and they went through together. She touched his arm. It felt solid. Down the hall, beyond the staircase, a door opened by itself. Behind them, the door to the master bedroom slammed and locked.

"What are you doing?" Nathan asked her.

"Me?" She looked behind her at the door. "They must have done it."

The doorknob rattled. Deirdre's voice said, "Let us out! Please, House. Susan? Are you all right? Nathan?"

"Me?" Susan repeated. Her breathing slowed. She touched the wall, felt that the house's breathing had slowed, too, and its pulse matched hers. As she stood, with the skull in her left hand and her right hand against the wall, she sensed the spaces and walls that made up the house. A structure built itself in her mind, misty walls that were not so much wood as skin and bone and energy, veins that pulsed with light. Her mind could close and lock a door as easily as she could close her hand into a fist. She sensed the knots and webs of energy that made up Edmund, Deirdre, and Julio, contained in the master bedroom, and the very different complex that was Nathan. Unlike the others, who were separate from everything around them, he was an extension of the house energies.

Terror and delight washed over her. She stroked her hand down the wall, and felt as though a warm hand pressed back. At home, she could tune in to the house, listen to its tiny sounds, sense its shifts, guess where people were and what they were doing by the sounds water made running in the bathroom sink, or the little tumbling catch and release when the flapper in the toilet tank didn't close all the way. She knew the sound each door made when it closed or opened. She knew the humming clicking that came from her father's typewriter in his office, and she could tell which window was open by how the air moved through the house.

This was so much better. Eyes closed, she leaned her cheek against the wall. There was a basement down there, and stacks, stacks of memories pressed into each wall, feelings and images, wonders and sadness. Everything that had ever happened inside, people, furniture, animals, celebrations, funerals, sleep and dreams; she could sense just the edges of them, for they were all folded away somehow, but she knew they could be opened up again, looked at. The house let her in, cradled her. Listened.

She stepped away from the wall. The sensations muted but did not disappear. "I'll be back," she said to Nathan, her voice tiny. "Tell them I'll be right back."

She went down the hall to the open door. Even with her back to Nathan, she was aware of his movements: he paused, then moved to the wall, merged with it, and disengaged himself inside the bedroom. A short scream from Deirdre. Then the murmur of conversation.

The room Susan entered was small. A tree leaned close to the window, its branches crooked as elbows. No furnishings hid the bare floorboards, and no pictures concealed any of the wallpaper, which bore a fading pattern of small blue ovals interrupting blue ribbons that ran from ceiling to floor. Susan waited. Presently a panel opened in the corner where the built-in closet met the wall. She crawled through into darkness until she bumped into something. Then she sat back to let light past her.

Tattered clothes still hung on the human frame, and a frayed rope still led away from the vertebrae of the neck. Susan wondered how the skeleton could have stayed here, undiscovered, for so long. She thought of flesh and rot and maggots; of smell. Horrible images flared through her mind. She shivered and buried them, the way she often buried dark thoughts. Everything had happened a long time ago. The bones were clean and naked now, no hint of flesh about them any longer.

Who had hidden him? Why?

The house must know.

Could she unfold this memory here? Touch the wall and slide a recollection out of it, look at something that had happened in the past?

Did she want to?

She set the skull on the floor beside the skeleton and sat a while, heedless of the dust. At last she said,

"House. I need one of these bones. I don't think I can touch him otherwise. Just a little one, to take with me everywhere." She waited a moment, sensing air currents. Without the skull in her hands, she couldn't sense the house as well, but she did sense tranquillity. She rubbed her eyes, then plucked at a small bone in the skeleton's right hand. There was a slight resistance, then it came away.

Fist closed tightly around the bone, she got to her feet and backed out of the tunnel. The panel slid shut, hiding the skeleton. She knocked on it; it made the muffled thunk of thick wood, and the seams were invisible. "Thank you," she whispered, and went back to the master bedroom. The door there opened at her touch.

Deirdre stopped speaking and looked at her, eyebrows up. Deirdre and Edmund sat on the bed. Julio stood with his back to the wall, and Nathan sat on the floor.

"I put the skull back," Susan said.

"I'm not sure about this house," said Deirdre. "I don't know if we ought to stay here. What if it locks us up for days?" She got up. "I'd like to get out while the getting's good." She made a dash for the door, but it slammed.

"Magic," whispered Edmund. Then, in a louder, wondering voice, "It's not all done with wires, is it? Is it magic, Nathan?"

"It's House." Nathan smiled. "No wires."

Deirdre wrestled with the doorknob. "How do you make it work? Why did it close? Why won't it open?"

Susan frowned. She touched Deirdre's shoulder. Deirdre moved aside, and Susan turned the doorknob. The door opened as though oiled.

"You can make it behave?" Deirdre asked.

"I don't know. I think so."

"I don't like you being in charge of everything."

"It's not like she planned it," said Julio.

Susan turned away. The bone in her hand was smaller than her sea stone, and lighter; it didn't feel natural there yet. "All for one, and one for all," she said to the wall. "Did that mean anything to you?" She faced Deirdre again. "It means we share what we have, doesn't it? I can open the doors, if the house lets me."

"Whenever I ask you to?"

"Yes."

"But what about just then, when you went away? I called you, and you didn't open the door."

Susan bit her lower lip. "I had to do that alone. That's all. I'm done now, okay?"

"But I don't *know* you. How can I trust you?"

"I know her," Julio said.

"How well? Do you trust her with your life?" Deirdre turned to Susan. "If I have to depend on you— I'm afraid. Don't you think that makes sense?"

A vision of power overwhelmed Susan. She imagined herself as the house, opening and closing doors at will, trapping people like playthings in one room or another, watching them scurry and rustle and rant. She could sit back and savor their distress, watch them grow weaker—free them if she pleased, or keep them if she cared to.

She wondered if her father felt that way about her and her mother.

"Yes," she said to Deirdre. "That makes sense." She gripped the doorknob, holding the door open. "Go. Go."

But Deirdre waited, staring into her face. "I don't think I have to," she said.

"What?"

"I trust you."

"Oh, no." Susan shook her head. "How can you?"

"That's all right, then," said Deirdre, half to herself. "Maybe this place will work out after all."

# chapter six

SUSAN FELT LIKE a real estate agent. She opened doors and stood back as the others went through them. Nothing they discovered in the rooms surprised her, though it all interested her.

Across the sitting room from the master bedroom, they found a large bathroom with a claw-footed tub, a sink on a pedestal, and a toilet with a wooden seat. A fringed carpet with red and pink flowers set in a large curlicued oval ran across the floor. The air smelled like air in a museum—not dead, but not lived in.

Around the corner from the bathroom, a door opened opposite the door to Nathan's room. Twin beds stood against the far wall, with a nightstand between them, and identical dressers supported mirrors that caught their images as they explored. The furniture was all honey-golden wood, and each piece had a carved scallop shell as a central decoration. Julio walked to the single desk and picked up a melon-backed mandolin. The arched ribs of the sound box alternated stripes of light and dark wood; edging the top and the sound hole were wood inlay and a strip of mother-of-pearl; mother-of-pearl vines climbed up the ebony neck beneath the frets. The instrument had no strings.

Julio held it out to Nathan.

"It belonged to one of my aunts," Nathan said. "I don't know which one. They were twins; they died before I was born. I've never seen strings on it. Do people still play mandolins?"

"Julio probably does," said Deirdre. "He plays anything." She tested a door in the corner of the room, then, when it refused to open, looked at Susan. Susan walked over and opened the door to reveal an empty closet. "This is silly," said Deirdre. "Why shouldn't I be able to open that door? Does the house only like beautiful girls?" She glared at Susan.

Susan walked into the closet and closed the door.

The darkness felt warm and safe, haunted by the fragrance of lavender sachet. She leaned against a wall, shutting out the memory of what Deirdre had just said. With her back to the wall and the bone in her hand, the misty mental map of the house opened to her, and she would have explored it, but Deirdre's pounding on the door was too insistent to shut out.

"Hey, I'm sorry. I always say dumb things. You have to learn to ignore it. Come on, Susan. Come out. Please. Okay, you have to come out, I want this door open, and you promised."

Susan hugged herself a little longer, making Deirdre's words into a string of no-meaning sounds, then opened the door, secure in her blankest smile, and came out. Would they all be looking at her again? Had she caused a scene?

Edmund wasn't even in the room, and Julio perched on one of the beds, still examining the mandolin. Nathan watched him.

"I'm sorry," Deirdre said again. "Yell at me or tell me to shut up. Everybody else does."

"I don't," said Susan.

"Maybe you can learn to," Deirdre said. "I'd feel better if you did. What's behind the door across the hall? I feel like I'm on a game show. Door number three, please."

Susan felt reluctant to open the door to Nathan's room, but she had promised. She turned the knob and gave the door a gentle push. It creaked as it opened. "Nathan's room," she murmured.

"This was *his* room? Ewww." Deirdre did not even step over the threshold, but Edmund came in. He stayed only seconds, then went out, shaking his head.

"What's behind this door?" he asked, going to a slender door between the top of the staircase and the master bedroom door.

Susan opened it, disclosing a set of tall narrow steps leading upward.

"This is spooky." Deirdre peered up into darkness.

"That's dumb," Edmund said. "If Nathan's the only ghost here, what have you got to be scared of?" To himself, he muttered. "Ghost. Ghost. I can't believe I said that and meant it. Wait. What am I talking about? I *do* believe it. This is so cool!"

Julio and Nathan rejoined them as Edmund fished a flashlight out of his backpack. After switching it on, he took the steps two at a time. At the top, he cried, "Oh," his voice a mingling of surprise and delight. Deirdre followed him up.

"I want *this* room," said Edmund as Susan and Julio stepped off the stairs. Rain made a constant, quiet patter on the roof above them. Raftered ceilings sloped nearly to the floor on two sides, and there was a large window in the third side across from the stairs. Edmund stood in the center of the hardwood floor, looking toward the window. Gray daylight touched his edges.

"Why doesn't this house leak?" Deirdre asked. "It looks so broken down from outside." She glanced up, and a drop landed on her nose. "Hey!" She squinted at the ceiling, but there was no follow-up. "See? You *can* cooperate if you like." She shook a finger at the ceiling.

Edmund turned back to them. "Can I have this room? Is that all right?" He looked at them all, but particularly at Nathan, who had come up silently to stand beside Susan.

"What do you want it for?" asked Nathan.

"It's perfect! It's perfect for my ceremonies." Edmund stared at Nathan. "There are five of us now," he said.

"What sort of ceremonies?"

"Edmund's been studying witchcraft," said Deirdre. At Edmund's glare, she ducked behind Julio.

"Witchcraft," Susan said. She cocked her head and stared at Edmund. She thought of the feather flower Edmund had produced for her in the library. But wasn't that a magic trick? Not what she thought of as witchcraft.

She had asked Edmund and Deirdre to trust her, even though they didn't know her. She didn't know them either, these two new people. Who *were* they?

"No. Magic." Edmund looked toward the window. "All right. Dee is right. Witchcraft. I've studied the kind of magic where you do tricks—" He pulled a quarter out of his pocket, made it spin on the end of his index finger, threw it up into the air; it caught light from the distant window, flashed, and dropped back into his hand. He snapped his fingers and the quarter vanished. "That wasn't what I really wanted. I wanted to figure out how to make things happen a different way, without wires and mirrors and tricks."

"So that's why we were looking for a place to do secret things," Julio said. "Edmund wants to try things he's read about in books, and for that we needed privacy and a big safe open space."

"Like this." Edmund pointed to the hardwood floor. "What I want to do takes space and five people. It might be really weird if one of us is a ghost, though." He frowned. "On the other hand, it might make it stronger. . . . We can start small, and see what happens."

"What are you trying to accomplish?" asked Nathan.

"Huh? Oh, nothing bad. I'm not trying to raise the dead or improve my grades or make somebody fall in love with me. But there are supposed to be things you can do to generate positive energy, and then direct it to where it's needed. I think that's safe. I don't think that will hurt people. I just want to see if it *works*."

The bone in Susan's hand tingled. The house was interested in this.

"That's fine with me," said Nathan. He glanced at the others, and they nodded. Susan hesitated, thinking about all the standard warnings in every scary book she had ever read, about not tampering with the unknown. She thought about fairy tales: Bluebeard's wife, who had to open the forbidden door; Pandora and her box; even Eve and the apple. She thought about saying no, backing out of this group, going home to silence.

Maybe if she did that, even Julio would desert her. And she didn't want to leave this house. "All right," she said at last.

"Then can I have a room, too?" said Deirdre. "What I want to do is private, too. Is that okay, Nathan?"

"It's fine with me."

"I'd like a music room," said Julio. "I live in a little apartment, and the neighbors don't like noise. I'd like a place to practice. Would that be okay?"

"We played music in the living room when I was

alive. It's downstairs, the big room with a fireplace," Nathan said.

"I've been thinking about that. It would be better if I used a room on the second floor. After all, I'll be making noise, and it would be better if people couldn't look right in and see me do it. Spookier. Maybe they'll think I'm part of the haunting if they can't see me. Or—could the house soundproof a room?"

Susan thought of the mental map she'd had of the house, its walls as skin and bone and muscle and energy. Could it thicken its own walls?"

"Maybe," Nathan said.

Julio smiled. "Would anybody mind if I took the twins' bedroom?"

"No," said Deirdre. She looked at Susan. "Do you want a room?"

"I don't have anything to do in a room," said Susan. Then she sensed Deirdre's dilemma. To be fair, everybody had to have a room, and the two rooms left on the second floor were the master bedroom and Nathan's room. "But I'll figure something out. I'll take Nathan's room." She glanced at Nathan. He looked a little worried, but he nodded.

"Oh, good," said Deirdre.

"I haven't even seen Nathan's room," Julio said. "Can I see it? I don't want it, it's just that I missed it on the tour."

"Come downstairs," said Susan.

"I'm going to set things up," Edmund said. He set

his backpack on the attic room's single piece of furniture, an old dresser, opened the pack's zippered pockets, and began unpacking.

"Do you want some of my furniture for your room, Susan?" Julio asked. "I've got double everything but the desk." He had come into Nathan's room, undisturbed by it, and gone out again.

"All right."

Everyone helped her move a bed and dresser into her room. Then they each went to their separate retreats and closed the doors.

"This was my father's room when he was a child before it was mine," Nathan told Susan. She sat on the bed, leaned against the headboard, and smiled at him. "His name was Nicholas. He liked the secret panel too."

"There's a lot of space behind the panel."

"It's like a room, only you can't stand up in it. It's the crawl space over the kitchen, and there's another entrance from the twins' bedroom. I have the feeling I don't need to tell you this. What have you got in your hand?"

She opened her hand and studied the small bone she held, showed it to him. "One of yours," she said after a pause. "I hope you don't mind."

"Why would you want a thing like that?"

She held out her hand to him. After a moment, he

came to her and touched her palm. She set the bone carefully on the bed beside her and held out her hand again. This time, his hand passed through hers—a chill, then nothing. His flesh had no more substance than a shadow.

"You're one of the only people I've ever touched," she said, "and you're not even really here. I want you to be here. Maybe that's not fair. I guess I should have asked you first. Is it all right?"

"It's all right."

She closed her hand around the bone again. "Do you ever play the 'you're me' game?"

"How does it work?" He sat at the foot of the bed.

"You look at people and think, 'You're me. Which part of me are you?' Then you watch them until you figure out what you have in common. It doesn't always work. I can't figure out what I have in common with Deirdre, for instance. But Nathan . . ."

"What?"

"You're me." She drew her knees up and hugged them. She swallowed. She hadn't meant to say it. She never told people what she was thinking. As she bent her head forward, her hair covered her face.

He lifted her hair aside and met her eyes. "But I'm dead, Susan."

"I know."

"You shouldn't be me."

She just looked at him, for a long moment. "I know." She turned away.

# chapter seven

SUSAN TAPPED ON the door of the master bedroom.

Deirdre opened the door. "See? It lets me work this now." She shut the door and opened it to demonstrate.

Susan grinned. "Okay. I have to go now. I told my father I was going to do research at the library, so I better do some. He'll expect to see my work."

Deirdre slid out of her room and shut the door. "Stay," she said to the doorknob. "Please." Then she turned to Susan. "I'll come with you."

"Why?" Susan asked, then smiled again and shook her head.

"Would you rather I didn't?"

"No. No, I'd like to have you." She looked at her fist. "Maybe that's why I knocked."

"I want to find out who you are," said Deirdre. "Julio knows you, but I don't."

"I don't know you either."

"Ask me anything. I might answer." Deirdre thumped down the stairs ahead of her.

Susan trailed her hand down the banister. Why couldn't she think of a good question?

Deirdre stopped in the dining room and lifted Susan's school bag from where she had dropped it earlier. "Jeez, what did you pack in here? Planning to go on vacation?"

"Some books, my notebook, pens, and an extra outfit in case I got this one dirty." Susan looked down at her skirt. It had dust smudges all over, and there was a rip in one of the pleats from a protruding nail head she'd run into while they were moving furniture.

"You're kidding. You *are* kidding, aren't you?"

Susan glanced at her, then held out her hand for the school bag.

"Nobody could be that stuck-up in real life," said Deirdre. "Hey, I saw you walk up and grab that skull. And *I* was screaming. I *never* thought I would do that. You're a lot braver than I am, which is *so* unfair." She opened the school bag's flap, peeked inside. "There *is* a dress. I know what it is. You have a secret identity."

Susan walked away. At the threshold of the back door, her left hand snagged on something. She glanced back and saw that it was trapped by air, trapped because she held the bone; like the skull, perhaps, it was not allowed to leave the house.

"Please," she whispered as Deirdre stared at her, questions in her eyes, on her lips: any minute an attack with more questions.

Susan pulled, and the house let go of her hand. The bone came outside with her.

She turned her back on Deirdre and went off through the brambles, heading for the woods. There was a path leading into the stand of alders and brambles. It ran down to a little creek in the bottom of the ravine.

Susan marched along without looking at her feet. She had left the sea stone on the stove again. But that was fair. She had traded one talisman for another.

She held a human bone in her hand, a piece of a dead person. A sudden shiver shook her. She opened her hand, peeked at the bone, shivered again. She curled her hand into a fist with the bone in the center. Deirdre thought she was brave. How brave was it to dip your toe in boiling water when you couldn't even feel it?

A piece of a dead person. Well, a piece of Nathan. Susan rubbed her thumb over the bone. Clean and dry and sanitary, not even dusty. She shivered once more, lifted her shoulders, relaxed.

Deirdre followed her, carrying the school bag. After crossing the creek, they reached a dirt road. Susan turned right, toward the highway. She walked on the grassy strip between the ruts, ignoring Deirdre, although she could hear the other girl behind her.

"All right, I'm sorry," Deirdre said as they reached pavement. They turned right, toward town and the library, away from Susan's father's house up on Shannon Hill. "I suppose you must have reasons for trying to be Miss Perfect."

Susan tucked her fist into her jacket pocket. They

reached the part of town where sidewalk and stores and restaurants started.

"How am I supposed to know? You have to talk to me if you want me to understand. I don't read minds," said Deirdre.

"I don't care whether you know or not."

"Yeah, but *I* care. If this is going to work, if we have to be friends, we can't be mad at each other all the time. I'm just being my normal insensitive self, and you're not used to me yet. Please talk to me."

"I have to look good when I get home," said Susan.

"Some kind of rule, huh?"

"That's right," Susan said. She shifted subjects. "How long have you known Julio and Edmund?"

"We all met in third grade. We were in the speed-readers' group. We've stuck together ever since, though this girl, Trudie, came close to breaking us up. Maybe that's why I'm nervous. Some people, you just can't tell about them. Julio introduced us to Trudie, too. Even *his* instincts aren't always good."

"I don't understand. This Trudie tried to break you up? Why would anybody do that?"

"Yeah, we don't get it either. She's just mean, though she acted really nice at first. We almost let her be our friend. We almost told her about Edmund. The witchcraft. That would have wrecked us at school, if Trudie told everyone about him. People already think we're weird, but— We've been suspicious ever since."

"No wonder," said Susan.

"But you're not going to tell."

"Of course not."

"I wish I knew I could trust you."

"You said you trusted me."

"Well, sorta." Deirdre hopped up on a bench in front of the Price Chopper IGA, walked along to its end, hopped down. "What was it with you and those doors, anyway? That house? I used to think Edmund was nuts, with this magic stuff, but those doors really opened and shut themselves. And Nathan walked through walls. God. I can't *believe* that happened." She shook her head. "Though I guess I want to believe. And I can't think of any other good explanation." She swung Susan's bag as she walked. "But it was still scary. When we did that Three Musketeers thing, I felt Nathan's hand on mine," she whispered.

"Mm."

"It was freezing."

"Mm."

"Quit saying that. It's *so* irritating!"

"Mm." Susan smiled.

Deirdre punched Susan's arm.

Susan froze. Her muscles locked. She couldn't move.

"What?" Deirdre asked.

Cold wrapped Susan's bones. A gust of wind swept her hair up, then released it.

"Susan?" Deirdre shook her arm. "Hey?"

The bone was warm in her hand. It glowed like an ember, sent out thaw.

"Hey! Are you all right? What happened?"

Thaw traveled up her arm, up her neck. It didn't reach her face, but it warmed her vocal cords. "Don't. Hit. Me." Each word puffed out on a separate breath, faint as a whisper, but harsh.

"All right. All right. Don't have a fit. I hit everybody. I didn't mean to hurt you."

"Don't."

"I'm sorry, okay? Jeez. What's the big deal?"

The thaw spread faster. Her skin tingled. Finally her knees unlocked. She took a step.

At home there was nothing she could do about people hitting people. Out here, where it was supposed to be safe, she didn't want anyone to hit her. Was it something she could control? She could try.

She shivered. The bone warmed the inside of her fist.

"So how weird are *you*?" Deirdre asked.

"I'm not weird." Susan took another step, relieved that she could move again.

Deirdre shook her head. "You're weird, all right. Like, what just happened to you? That wasn't normal. And you can talk to the haunted house, and it listens to you. Besides, you look like the perfect goody-goody girl, just the kind of girl my mother wishes I would be, and you're braver than I am. That makes me sick! How could you just grab a skull off the floor?"

"I thought it was fake," said Susan.

"How could you *think* when everything happened so fast?"

Susan shrugged.

"I hate that," Deirdre grumbled. "But, on the other hand, it's something I admire about you. But then there's the statue thing that just happened." She sighed. "This is going to take work."

# chapter eight

SUSAN WOKE ON Monday feeling there was a bubble inside her—a rainbow iridescence enclosing something lighter than air. It puzzled her. Then she remembered. She had found two keys to happiness.

The first was her Science Question.

After Deirdre left her, Susan had visited the library and found magazine articles that mentioned video games as the most obvious manifestation of computers in people's lives so far. She decided her question was: *How do video games change people's personalities?*

She'd checked the phone book, left the library, and headed along the highway. There was a little video arcade downtown, a dark alcove between a candy store and a souvenir shop. It had sticky floors, and most of the light in it came from the game screens. *Beeps, zisses, pi-yows*, strange small snatches of music, and boys' curses and threats flew through the air.

At first she was afraid to go in, but she gripped Nathan's bone and entered.

The arcade was warm and smelled like people who

hadn't bathed recently. She watched people play for a while. Eventually she introduced herself to five of the regulars, all teenage boys. She couldn't believe she could go up to strangers, most of them older than she was, and just start talking to them, but somehow, she managed. Maybe it helped to have the bone. Maybe it helped that she had a mission.

She waited quietly while they played, and only talked to them between games, while they were waiting for someone else to wipe out so they could get back on their favorite machines. Then they were perfectly willing to tell her anything. She took copious notes. From the way they dropped their gazes and fidgeted, she guessed they weren't used to talking to girls, any more than she was used to talking to anybody.

She asked them questions about who they were, how long they'd been playing, and how they felt it had changed them. Most of the players told her they had gotten a lot better at shooting space invaders, or knocking the middles out of centipedes, or chomping blue dots while running away from ghosts, or climbing ladders and jumping over barrels.

Barrel jumping?

One of them treated her to a game of Donkey Kong.

She hesitated, afraid to touch something so many other people had touched, the buttons to make Mario jump, the joystick to move him forward, up, down, all greasy with the caresses of others before her. But then she told herself: *It's research.*

She had to tuck Nathan's bone in her pocket to play. She remembered she had touched other and stranger things without thinking twice.

She surprised herself laughing. The music, the little man with the mustache, the bunches of bananas. It was silly and fun.

One boy, Richie, had only started playing that week. He got killed quickly in every game he played. One of the other boys, Mark, was mentoring him, teaching him secrets to gaining power and avoiding traps. Richie and Mark were perfect subjects for Susan's research. She could watch Richie to see how he changed. Both of them said they came to the arcade every day after school, and they wouldn't mind talking to her.

She started several different pages in her notebook for data collection, and went home happy. Not only did she have her project, she had a reason to go downtown instead of home after school every day. Observation! Data collection.

That night at dinner, she told her father she needed to do research for a month, every day except Sunday. She was afraid to ask for more time than that. She would have to gather data, graph it, and build a display for her project for the Science Fair in November. After that, maybe she could come up with another reason not to go right home after school.

The haunted house was her second key to happiness. She could go to the arcade for half an hour every day and collect data—she had told Father that she wanted to watch how people changed over time in their relationship with computers, which meant a lot of observation—and then stop at the haunted house before she went home.

Now her day had a direction to it. Everything leaned toward the three hours between school and supper. She wasn't sure what she wanted to do with her room at the house yet, but just knowing it was there gave her a strange and unfamiliar feeling of security.

She sat up in bed, hugged her knees, and looked around her room, wondering if there was anything she could take to the house to make Nathan's room more hers.

There was a horrid perfection to her room, from its dusty-rose carpet to the three antique porcelain dolls on the gold-and-white shelf above her desk. She had never been allowed to play with the dolls; they had been given to her when she was young enough to break them, and by the time she was old enough to touch them, she had lost the desire.

She got up and went to her gold-and-white vanity, lowered her eyes so she didn't see her reflection. A mother-of-pearl-backed brush lay beside a tortoise-shell comb, next to a cut-crystal dressing-table set. Susan opened the satin-topped jewelry box and looked at the strand of seed pearls and the tiny silver ring with its silver rose Father had given her for different birthdays. He had thrown away her favorite piece of jewelry, a Cracker Jack ring with a green plastic stone that Julio had given her when they were seven.

She hung up her nightgown and dressed quickly, feeling as if she couldn't breathe, even with the windows the regulation inch-at-the-bottom open. She grabbed her school bag and Nathan's bone from her desk.

Father and Mother were at breakfast at the kitchen table. Mother looked sleepy, her head propped on her hand, blonde hair half covering her face. A menthol cigarette smoked itself in the mother-of-pearl holder in her other hand. Susan said, "Good morning," and sat at her place, noticing that all the silverware was neatly and precisely aligned. Mother must have had a good night.

"You didn't comb your hair," Father said.

Oh, no. Susan put her hands in her lap and closed her eyes while Father got the comb. She reminded herself she didn't feel pain. By the time he finished pulling the snags out, her eyes were open. She watched him with detachment.

"That's my girl," he said, and smiled at her. "That's my fairy princess."

She held the bone tight in her left hand and picked at her eggs with a fork. Scrambled eggs were the only kind Mother knew how to make; they had scrambled eggs four mornings a week and cereal the other three. Susan's stomach had tightened too much for her to eat.

"Drink your juice," said Father.

She obeyed, watching him over the rim of her glass. Sometimes she thought of him as a property owner. He

owned her image, her hair and teeth and skin, everything people saw when they looked at her; he owned her
presence. He made the rules about what clothes she
wore, how long her hair was, how clean she had to keep
herself. He made the rules about where she had to be
and when. She couldn't fight him.

But her brain and all the landscapes and architec-
ture in it belonged to her.

Below the edge of the table, she lifted her skirt three
inches and peeked at her bruise. Over the weekend, it
had lightened to olive green ringed with yellow. She
could damage part of his property and he would never
know. She savored the tiny revenge.

She left the house before her father did.

Relieved, she drew in deep lungfuls of sea-scented
air, touched the fuzz on the leaves of a thimbleberry
bush, felt her school bag bumping her side as she walked.

In the town below, sudden hazy sun illuminated
evergreens, angles of buildings, windows, lush lawns.
She walked down the hill, watching clouds over the
ocean. South, rain hung like gauze between clouds and
sea. Where the horizon met the sky, the sea made a line
of midnight blue, and the sun scattered silver lace on
the water, now close to shore, now far away.

Susan drifted through the school day like the some-
time sun, touching down in each class, then vanishing
into fogged thoughts. French, English, history passed;
lunch and recess. Math engaged her. Field hockey woke
her up.

After school, she headed downtown. There were so many things she could have been doing downtown all these years instead of staying home. Suppose she went to the DairyMaid and bought an ice-cream cone and ate it while watching everyone else? Last week she would have thought she'd hate to do that. This week she wasn't sure.

Suppose she went to the beach all by herself? She didn't have to go all the way down to the sand. She could stand up on the cliffs and watch the waves scrolling in, and people walking on the sand, and the way silver mist beat up to cloak the distances along the coast.

The haunted house was the best suppose of all.

But first she went to the arcade. The manager, a thin dark man with sparse hair, prominent forehead veins, and an apron with pockets full of quarters, quizzed her about her intentions. She explained her science project to him, and he said it would be all right, as long as she spent at least a dollar in the arcade with every visit. A dollar? She still had money from a birthday check her uncle Henry had sent her. Four games. She could play four games every day, at least until her money ran out.

Richie, the guy who had just started playing, tried to tutor her, but he got killed even faster than she did.

She would observe herself, too, she decided. Would playing video games change her in any observable way? Would she be able to tell, watching from inside herself? She could call herself Subject X. Maybe she should devise some kind of attitude test and give it to all her subjects, then retest toward the end. Maybe her Science Question was too open-ended; maybe she should be looking for particular results. If people changed, what direction did they change in? She couldn't guess yet what to watch for.

She played four games of Centipede, logged her feelings afterward (frustration, excitement, a little dizziness), checked with each of her other subjects, made a few more notes, then left, walking fast toward Lee Street.

❧

The bone in her hand warmed as she rounded the house. The back door opened before she touched it.

She stepped inside, walked the hall to the kitchen, and touched the wall. She saw double: dusty gray walls with peeling strips of old wallpaper hanging off them, scratched wooden counters, rust-spotted black stove (her sea stone still sat on it), brown floor dulled with the varnish of age and reality, while just under the surface lurked webs of light, tendons of energy. The house's breathing shifted to match hers, and she knew that Julio, Edmund, and Deirdre were already there.

"Nathan?" she said.

A shadow inked itself across the floor, long and spidery, and then a form shimmered into a position to cast it. He smiled.

"I like that," she said.

"Deirdre screamed. Then she said it was good

special effects. I suppose that means what it sounds like. Susan, I went out on the porch today!"

"Did anyone see you?"

"I didn't care. It is the first step I've taken out of House—other than on Halloween—since I died."

She looked at the bone in her hand, then at him. "So something is changing. My taking the bone out of the house—you think that did it?"

"Yes."

"What happens on Halloween? That's next week."

"On All Hallows' Eve, all the ghosts in the world are loosed from whatever binds them to particular places. Not all of them know it. Some don't care. I still don't really understand ghosts; some are people, some are monsters, and some are just shadows of people. On Halloween, I go out and roam the world. There are things to learn, strange things to watch, people to scare. Do you ̖un around in a costume like others in the United States do these days? Shall I come with you?"

"I'm not allowed out on Halloween," she said. She had seen trick-or-treating on TV shows, and heard people talking about it the day after Halloween at school. She didn't really get it, but she had always wished she could go. Only what would she dress up as? She had her fancy clothes for Father's events and her school clothes. When she was little, she had had a few play outfits. Suppose she wore one of Father's suits?

She shivered.

In a whisper that was a wish, she said, "Come visit me."

In a whisper that was a promise, Nathan said, "I will."

She held his bone against her cheek and smiled at him. He smiled back, his eyes vivid blue in his pale face. His was the most beautiful face she had ever seen— shadowed eyes, the transparency at the outer edges of him. Her heart spoke in her ears. At last she couldn't look at him any longer; they turned away at the same moment. Sour and sweet lay on her tongue.

She went through the dining room to the staircase, then upstairs.

Fragments of melody leaked from Julio's room. Susan knocked on his door. He opened it. He held the mandolin, which now had strings.

He grinned and invited her in. "Do you still play piano?"

"Badly." Father had stopped the lessons when she reached twelve and showed no promise of improving.

"That's all right, I don't have a portable one any- way. Listen to this." He sat on the bed and picked out a melody on the mandolin. It sounded old and nonclassi- cal. "I talked to Barry at the music store. Mandolin fin- gering is just like violin, only with frets. But the pick- ing—" He looked at the pick he held between the thumb and index finger of his right hand. "I listened to a couple records. It's sort of like shivering. I have to practice."

"What was that tune? Do it again." Susan put her

coat and school bag on his bed. She watched his fingers as he played.

"It's called 'Over the Waterfall.' I think it's a very old tune. I don't know where I first heard it. I hear these songs in my dreams sometimes."

"Does that one have words?"

"Not that I ever heard. You still sing?"

"In church," she said. Her voice was high and pure, one of the few things about herself she actually liked.

"I'd like to play music with other people, but I don't know if any of you want to work with me. Deirdre's not a natural musician, and neither is Edmund. I wonder if Nathan plays an instrument? I wonder if he *can* play an instrument? Have you figured out what you're going to do in your room?"

"Just knowing it's there is enough. I thought maybe I could put some of my own things in it, but I haven't found anything I like yet. Maybe my sea stone?" The sea stone was payment for Nathan's bone, but the house probably wouldn't care where she left it, as long as it was inside. She rose and went to a window, one of the ones that looked out over Lee Street. The curtains had frayed into long snarled tassels of silk. Below in the yard, mounded castles of blackberry cane stood, rich dark green, a few berries still showing shiny ripe, others meshed in gray web.

A red-haired girl stepped from the road onto the thin ribbon of path that snaked through the yard.

"Look," Susan said to Julio.

The stranger seemed to hear Susan. She raised her head.

Julio glanced out the window, then grabbed Susan and pulled her to the floor.

"Do you know her?" Susan asked.

"That girl?" he whispered. "It's Trudie. Keep your voice down. I hope she didn't see you. Maybe Nathan can scare her away. Maybe she won't come any closer. Oh, she'll come closer. It's Trudie. She always comes closer."

"Are you all right?"

He crept to the door and closed it. "Maybe the house can lock all the doors. Is that something you can ask it to do? Trudie wouldn't break a window—or would she? You know what we need? Intercoms. I wish I could tell Dee—"

Nathan seeped up through the floor. "What do you want to tell her?"

"*¡Madre de—!* Oh, it's you. There's this girl outside, Nathan. Her name is Trudie. Can you tell Dee and Edmund that? It's sort of an emergency."

"All right." He drifted toward the inside wall.

"Why can't we tell them ourselves? She can't see through walls, can she?" asked Susan.

"She'd know. She's like that. X-ray hearing or something."

"What's so bad about Trudie?" Susan remembered what Deirdre had said, but she wanted to hear Julio's version.

"She's just—terrible. She's devious and mean," he

whispered. "She tries to wreck anything she can't have. She came to our school a couple years ago, and saw we were friends, and I bet she decided right then to pit us against each other. For a while we didn't understand. She acted like our friend. She was nicer to us than we were to each other, and I think we fell a little in love with her—at least, Edmund and I did; Deirdre thought she'd found a new best friend. Trudie is so sneaky. She would just drip a little poison here, a little there. We resented each other without knowing why. We had fights. We spent whole weekends not speaking to each other. Then we got together and compared notes. Now we're on our guard. . . . I bet she followed one of us." He crept back to the window and peeked over the sill.

Susan joined him. The redhead had come closer. She raised her head and turned it, nose to the air as if trying to catch scents. She had a broad, homely face and masses of curly auburn hair. Her green eyes were bright as bottle glass.

Julio and Susan ducked.

"She'll never leave this place alone if she thinks we're in it," said Julio.

"I shall go downstairs," said Susan. She backed away from the window and stood up, touched the door, which opened. "I *am* the lady of the house," she murmured.

Nathan joined her on the stairs. They walked down together.

# chapter nine

WITH EACH STEP she took, Susan felt the house's presence more strongly. Serenity seeped into her, the product of another age. At the same time, she was changing. Her skin tingled. The bone was hot in her hand. Something felt different about the way her hem brushed her knees. She paused at the base of the stairs and looked down.

She was wearing a navy blue sailor dress, with white trim on broad cuffs, hem, and wide collar. The dress nipped in at the waist, and the knee-length skirt had sharp pleats. Black stockings gloved her legs, and her shoes had turned to black high-button boots.

Definitely not the outfit she'd put on that morning.

Nathan studied her. She realized that they both looked like old-fashioned schoolchildren.

She held out her hand. He took it. His hand was chilly, his grip firm.

At the base of the stairs, she glanced toward the dining room on her left. Weren't there possibilities whispering to each other in the dusty room? They nudged her, and she nodded.

Shadows of turn-of-the-century furniture filled the dining room. They acquired weight and color. The long table took on the dark honey hue of polished oak, and the tall-backed chairs around it glowed with the same warm richness. Atop the table, a silver ornamental centerpiece and elaborate silver candlesticks took shape. The curls of stained and dusty wallpaper vanished as the walls reclaimed color and freshness.

Susan and Nathan walked along the front hall toward the big front door. Susan hadn't yet seen this part of the house. On her right, a broad double doorway gave entrance to the living room. Images shimmered into sight: on a red-and-blue carpet, a strange rectangular piano stood, and a golden harp with a three-legged stool beside it, overstuffed chairs and ottomans, and little tables with scattered knickknacks and pots of flowers. On the mantel, silver candlesticks flanked a large bronze-and-marble clock, and a portrait hung above—a lady in a mint-green dress with white flowers embroidered on it.

"Is this how the room used to look?" Susan asked.

"Yes," said Nathan, his tone rising.

Side by side they passed the living room on the right, a door into a dark room on the left. They reached the front door. Susan released Nathan's hand, grasped the crystal knob, and turned it.

Trudie stood on the front porch. Her eyes widened.

"Yes?" said Susan. "May we help you?"

"What?"

"You appear to have found your way to our front porch." Susan felt Mother's best Imperial Mood sweep into her, a mixture of kindness and condescension. "Did you have a specific reason for that, or would you care to find your way back to the street?"

"What?" Trudie swallowed. "Do you live here?"

"In spirit," Susan said.

Trudie cast a frightened glance at Susan's clothes.

Susan stared at Trudie and raised her eyebrows.

"Can—can I come in?"

"I'm sorry," said Susan. "We haven't been properly introduced." She closed the door. Then she took a deep breath and stared at Nathan.

Unholy delight filled her. She grinned at him, and he smiled back, his eyes alight. She had never played a trick on anyone before. She couldn't have conceived of it, let alone managed all the details. And yet, somehow—

The house roused them a moment later.

Susan let house awareness fill her. She felt how the walls interlocked, how the heating pipes, plumbing, and what wiring there was snaked between inner and outer walls. She sensed the symmetry of beams and rafters, the snake-scale overlap of shingles, the interrupted embrace of windows and doors. Again, she was aware of Nathan as a complex of tangled energies half-submerged in the floor, and of how the images of furniture were like him, though much less intricate. In this strange, huge array of space and solid, she sensed her friends, three warmer fields of energy, knots grouped together at the top of the stairs.

And on the porch—another warm knot, moving toward the living room window.

Susan opened the door again. "I beg your pardon, but you are being unmannerly," she said to Trudie, who straightened from her guilty stoop, looked over her shoulder at Susan, and flushed.

"I only wanted to see—you have such lovely furniture—could I—could I have a glass of water?"

"Our pump is out of order," said Susan.

"Doesn't he talk?" Trudie pointed a thumb at Nathan.

"I advise you to leave before anything worse happens," Nathan said.

Trudie put her hands on her hips and smiled a mean smile. "What could be worse than you two?"

"Oh," said Susan, "it depends on what you're afraid of."

"You don't scare me. Two kids in prissy outfits. Halloween isn't until next week. What kind of joke is this?" She reached out and pinched Susan's cheek. "You're as alive as I am."

Nathan's eyes grew enormous, their blue darkening to vivid turquoise. He lifted a hand, the fingers spread wide, and pushed it toward Trudie's face. She stared at it, mesmerized, as it came closer. Reflex closed her eyes, but she opened them again when the expected touch did not come—opened them and saw him pull his hand out of her head.

She stood on the porch and opened her mouth. A scream poured out.

Susan felt her cheeks prickle with departing blood. The noise was so awful. Nathan faded from sight. Susan backed away from the screaming girl, and the door slammed of its own accord.

Susan ran for the stairs, hurtled up them, and bumped into Edmund, Julio, and Deirdre.

The scream cut off. Thudding footsteps sounded from the front porch.

"What happened?" Deirdre asked before they untangled themselves.

"I think we scared her," said Susan. She was shivering. She hugged herself.

"I think you scared *you*," Deirdre said. "Are you all right?"

"Give me a minute." Susan sat on the stairs, and the others sat around her. She closed her eyes. Deirdre gripped her shoulder. Shivers quaked through Susan. Deirdre's hand was steady and warm and comforting.

Susan tried to feel with her house sense: Where was Nathan? Where was Trudie? Was the furniture still downstairs? Her house awareness had abandoned her.

"Where did you get those clothes?" Julio asked. "It's not what you were wearing when you went downstairs."

Susan opened her eyes and looked at the box pleats of her dark blue skirt. She pinched the fabric. It felt like good cotton cloth. "I don't know," she said. "I think they're ghost clothes. Maybe they'll disappear."

"Do you know your hair is tied back with a big fat white ribbon?" asked Deirdre.

"I'm not surprised. I wonder what happened to my real clothes. Maybe they're under these—?" She patted her chest—no feeling of layers under the new clothes, no sign of what she'd dressed in that morning—then realized she had dropped Nathan's bone in the confusion. "Oh, that must have something to do with it." She struggled to her feet. "Excuse me a minute."

"Wait. Where are you going?" asked Edmund.

"I lost something in the front hall. I'll be right back."

Deirdre caught Susan's ankle before she could start down the stairs. "Be careful," she said. "Trudie might still be around."

Susan nodded, and stayed close to the edges of the stairs to minimize creaking as she went down.

The dining room had become an empty acre of dusty floor again, ill lit by what light could force its way through the grimy double window. The living room stood empty. Susan knelt in the front hall. After a short search, she found the bone; it had rolled under the window seat in the round, downstairs tower room. She closed her hand around the bone with great relief. "Nathan?" she said.

"Are you still speaking to me?" His voice came from the air.

"Oh, Nathan," she said softly. She waited, stooping, using one hand to steady herself. After a moment he took shape.

She searched his face, then smiled. "It was wonderful," she said. "Scary, and wonderful."

"How can you say that?"

"You defended me," she whispered.

"I abandoned you."

"Not when I needed you. I dropped your bone, anyway. I'm sorry. I didn't mean to."

He smiled. "It didn't hurt." He helped her to her feet.

"Is she still around? I can't tell anymore." She paused and tested her own statement. With the bone in her hand, she came back into house awareness, and the awareness extended out into the yard, climbing blackberry brambles and red alders and the scrubby shore pines that leaned toward the house. Trudie was not in range, though the brambles bore traces of her passage—threads from her shirt and a few drops of blood where the thorns had scratched her. She had trampled some brambles in flight. The canes were straightening.

"So she ran," Susan whispered. "Good."

Deirdre tiptoed down the hall. "She gone?" she whispered.

"Yep," said Susan.

"You can come out now," Deirdre said over her shoulder, and Julio and Edmund came forward.

Susan giggled. "Just like the Munchkins."

"They want to know: are you a good witch, or a bad witch?"

Susan laughed.

"No, really," said Edmund.

Something in his tone sobered her. She stared at them.

"You've been consistently weird about all this," Edmund said, "accepting every strange and unbelievable thing that comes along. There's magic here, real magic, the kind I've been searching for all my life. We found it! I always wanted to believe, but I was never sure until now. The last two nights I kept waking up, thinking, was everything that happened at the haunted house a dream? Oh, God, it was real! It's real. But it doesn't surprise *you*. *Are* you a witch?"

"I'm not even sure I believe in them. I'm waiting to see what you turn into. Does it take one to know one?"

"I'm not kidding, Susan," he said.

Both of her hands tightened into fists. "If I were a witch," she said, "I would—I would—" There were so many things she would change! Could spells tie people up? Paralyze them? Keep their mouths shut and their arms helpless, maybe forever?

The ferocity of her impulses upset her.

Something clicked in her head, and her rage vanished. She glanced at her watch. "Oh, dear. Look at the time. I have to go home."

"Wait a minute," said Deirdre.

Susan's thoughts scattered and melted. "I have to go," she said again. "I have to. Julio—"

"I'll walk you home," he said. "Just a minute while I get my things."

🌱

Her clothes changed as she stepped over the threshold of the back door. Her hair fell loosely to her shoulders, and the navy dress faded into the combination of clothes she had dressed in that morning, a white blouse, a forest-green skirt, navy knee socks, and loafers. She felt the gathering chill in the air and remembered she had left her blazer and school bag in Julio's room. She glanced back. He brought her things with him.

"Thank you," she said as Julio handed her her coat. She put it on.

"You're welcome. But Susan, you're going to have to answer questions sooner or later."

"They were just teasing, weren't they? I don't know how to deal with that. I'm sorry. I don't want to get you in trouble with your friends—" Her mother's placating voice, trying to smooth things over.

"Stop it," he said.

"Stop what?"

"You can't make everything go away by ignoring it or pretending you're not who you are."

Couldn't she? She shifted from one foot to the other and looked at her watch. "This is nonsense," she said in her father's voice.

He dropped her school bag and took her shoulders. "Susan. Stop. Stop fighting. What time does your father get home tonight?"

"Five-thirty." She tried to lift her wrist and look at her watch again. She had been staring at it without seeing it.

"It's only four-fifteen now. There's plenty of time. Stop running away, Susan."

She stood still, but everything in her urged flight.
People would ask unanswerable questions. Her mind
was a minefield, full of places she dared not step.
"Remember, Princess," whispered her father's voice,
"we don't air our dirty linen in public. Whatever happens, let's keep it at home. That's what Family means.
We take care of it ourselves."

The questions wouldn't be about what happened at
home. The people in the house just wanted to talk about
magic. There was no magic at home. She had nothing to
worry about.

Wrong. Somehow it was all connected.

Julio, who usually defended her, was now on the
attack. Here she was, out in the open. She could run,
but he knew where she lived. She could run, but the
problems would follow.

She could stay, and let things wash over her without
effect. Click! Her mind could shunt everything off into
darkness.

All sensation faded from her skin inward. After a
moment, she couldn't even feel the bone in her hand.
She waited.

Julio shook her a little. "Please don't do that. Don't
go away behind your eyes. Talk to me. I'm your friend."

Tingles invaded her left hand, radiating from the
bone. They were warm; they climbed up her arm. She
knew it was the house trying to rouse her. It worked
through her, opening her house sense; she could almost
hear the house speak. It said that if she abandoned the

structure of her body, the house would be willing to take it over—dress it, animate it, bind it tight to this location. She could be another of its ghosts.

Part of her wanted that, with a horrible dark joy: to abdicate responsibility, act on the orders of something other than her father, leave her mother to fend for herself. Never to worry because her mother was hostage for her behavior. Never to feel shackles binding her movements whenever her father was at home. Never to struggle for a calm facade in a social situation again.

And she would never have to be alone again. Nathan was here. . . . Where was he? She used house sense to search. He was everywhere, and nowhere—spread thin throughout the house.

"Susan," said Julio. His fingers tightened on her shoulders. She could feel again.

She couldn't leave her mother alone up on Shannon Hill. Father would come home, find Mother there, and no Susan. He would reach for the heavy silver hairbrush.

"What do you want?" she asked Julio. She felt exhausted.

"Answer some questions."

"All right."

"Come back inside."

"All right." She let him lead her into the house.

# chapter ten

"THE DOORS OPENED for you, and they wouldn't for us," said Deirdre, "though they've gotten more ordinary lately. Then those clothes. And scaring Trudie—what did you do? What else *can* you do?"

Susan sat on the bed in Julio's room, her hands loose in her lap. Everyone else was ranged around the room, Julio perched on the dresser, Deirdre near her on the bed, Edmund to her other side.

After a moment, Susan held up her left hand, open, with the bone on her palm. "I don't know how it works. This is a bone from Nathan's hand." She looked at Edmund, wondering if his research gave him insight into this. He was intrigued, but he didn't appear to have anything to say. "When I hold this, I can—it's like I can see everywhere in the house, only it's not seeing, just a kind of knowing. House is a person, and it lets me—it's like it lets me use its senses. I'm terrible at explaining things." She touched her mouth with her right hand. "I listen to my house at home a lot. Kind of like tuning in a radio station, getting past the static? When I listen really hard, I can sense where other people are in it, and that's important."

"Why?" asked Deirdre.

Susan hesitated. It was easier to talk than she had expected, but this was a central secret, and there was a lock on it.

When she was a baby, she had had Nana, because Mother didn't know how to take care of her. Nana was one of the few comfortable people Susan had ever known. But when Susan was five, Nana had yelled at Father. "You should be reported to the police," she had yelled. "You should be locked up."

Then Nana disappeared. Susan had cried a long time that night, waiting for Nana to come in and comfort her, but Nana had not come, so she cried herself to sleep.

The next morning her tall, shiny father had taken her hand and led her into her mother's room. "Look, Fairy Princess," he said, setting her gently on Mother's bed and turning back the covers. "Look what happens to Mother when Princess cries."

She hadn't known what a bruise was. She had touched the purple place on Mother's arm, seen the pain in Mother's eyes, a sad, silent pain.

"It hurts Mother when you cry," Father had explained.

Susan had learned to be very quiet.

She thought for a long time that her sobs made the bruises appear, brought to blossom the purple hurt places on her mother that, when touched, made her mother flinch. Mostly the bruises were somewhere Mother could hide them, her arms, her back, her legs. Invisible when Mother was dressed in long-sleeved blouses and slacks, detectable only by the way Mother walked, the way her shoulders bent. Susan had swallowed sobs, smothered them in pillows, learned to send pain somewhere else.

Later, when Susan understood that Father was the one who made the bruises on Mother whenever Susan did something he didn't like, she had learned how to behave, what to wear, what not to do, and what never to talk about.

"I just have to know where people are," Susan told Deirdre.

"Where's Nathan?" asked Julio.

"Everywhere. Nathan?" She closed her hand on the bone, reached out with her house sense. He materialized by the window.

"Jeez," said Deirdre to him. "I keep forgetting you can do things like that. Do you know how Susan does what she does?"

"No. I don't understand any of this. All I know is that I almost feel alive."

"If I held your bone, what would happen?" Edmund asked.

"Try it."

Susan set the bone in Edmund's hand. Her house sense damped down, though not completely. She watched Edmund's face, waited for new awareness to dawn. He closed his eyes. After a moment, he opened them, shaking his head. "Nothing," he said. "Nathan, did it make a difference to you?"

"Not much." Nathan walked over. "When Susan holds the bone, I can touch her."

Edmund stretched out his hand, and Nathan touched his palm. The ghost's fingers stopped at Edmund's skin. "Wow," said Edmund.

"That worked with the skull, too," Deirdre said. "When we said the Musketeers oath."

"Huh. You could feel his hand?"

"Oh, yeah." She shivered. "Freezing."

"It's strange, but neat."

Nathan grinned, made a fist, knocked on Edmund's forehead.

"Come in," Edmund said in a door-answering voice.

"Can't do that as long as you're holding the bone."

"You mean, if I put this down, you can—come in?"

Nathan stepped back. "I don't know."

They stared at each other, puzzled.

Edmund curled his fingers around the bone. "I wonder if it gives me other powers." He stared at the door. "Door, close."

"It doesn't work like that!" Susan cried. The door slammed shut. "You can't order House around."

"Door, open," said Edmund. Nothing happened. "It worked the first time." He frowned.

"No," said Susan. "House closed the door because it wanted to. You can't order House around."

Edmund went to the door and turned the knob. He

rattled it and tugged on it. "How are we going to get out?"

"Humbly beseech it," Susan said.

"House, please let me open the door." Edmund waited a moment, then turned the knob. The door remained closed.

"Do I get down on my knees?" he asked Susan.

She rose and laid her hand on the door. The house-pulse tingled in it, along with buried laughter. The door swung open. She glanced at the others. Edmund wore the face of an experimenter, interested in any results. Deirdre leaned against the bed, arms crossed over her chest, a frown on her face. Julio smiled, and Nathan just waited.

"Works with or without the bone," said Edmund.

"There's something special about you, Susan. You can't deny it anymore," Julio said.

"Am I a witch?" Her throat felt tight again, and her stomach hurt.

"It doesn't mean you're a witch," said Edmund. "Maybe you're psychic."

"Does that mean mind reading? I can't read people's minds."

"There are lots of different ways to be psychic," Edmund said.

Susan's shoulders tightened and twisted. She buried her hands in her skirt pockets.

"What's psychic about conjuring up clothes?" asked Deirdre.

"House did that. I've never worn clothes like that."

"But it's more complicated than that," said Nathan. "You needed the clothes, and House supplied them. You looked for furniture, and House gave you furniture."

"Furniture?" Edmund said.

"She refurnished the downstairs just the way it was when my mother was alive. Things I sold were there," said Nathan. There was hunger in his voice. "She's almost a better ghost than I am." He stared at her, his eyes wide.

"Furniture. Can you do it again?" Julio asked.

Susan checked her watch. This time she saw it. Almost five, and she wanted to get home early enough to settle in before Mother and Father arrived. "I really do have to go, this time." She held out her hand to Edmund. "May I have the bone back, please?"

"Even though it doesn't affect what you can do?"

"It affects everything. It's my talisman. Besides, Nathan and I are conducting an experiment with it. I took it outside, and then he could go outside, too. Maybe we can get that to work even more."

Edmund gave her the bone.

"Eww. How can you play with bones?" Deirdre asked. "That's what *I* think is strange about you. You don't notice what you can do, and you play with bones. Hasn't anyone ever told you you're weird?"

"I hope nobody else ever noticed. I've never done these things before." She touched the wall. The house felt warm. She wondered if there had always been something special about her that had waited to wake up until she got here, or if being here had made her special.

"I'll talk to you tomorrow, all right?" she said.

"All right," said Deirdre.

Juanita had left a pan of enchiladas in the refrigerator, along with a tossed green salad that Mother would marinate in salad dressing later. Father disliked enchiladas; he disliked what he called "messy food," food that dripped when you cut into it. Juanita said she would cook what she liked, or leave. She was the only person Susan had ever seen stand up to Father and win.

Susan had hidden in the hall closet to hear this fight, which happened when she was eight. Juanita was the tenth housekeeper they'd had since Nana left, and Susan's favorite of all those who had come and gone, partly because of Julio, who had come to the house with his mother.

During the food fight, Father had yelled, and Juanita had yelled back. Father had talked about ruining people—at the time, Susan hadn't known what that meant, and she still wasn't too sure; she only knew it sounded mean and scary—and Juanita had yelled back: "You're not the only one can ruin someone with talk, Mr. Backstrom. People already talking about you, all the ones you fired. You get rid of me and nobody else will ever work for you."

Juanita stayed on, and cooked what she liked.

There was nothing in the kitchen Mother wouldn't be able to handle, so Susan went upstairs.

She rolled typing paper into the IBM Selectric typewriter her father had given her when his office upgraded to newer models. She set special tabs and typed up the day's observations from the arcade. She got graph paper and made a column for each person she was observing, then wrote general behaviors down the side and put X's in the columns where she had observed people doing them.

The project was shaping up. It looked scientific, even though what she was doing was pretty soft science. Subjects: R (for Richie), D (for Doug), M (for Mark), W (for Will), and X (for herself). Behaviors: "Shuts down awareness of anything but the computer monitor (gauged by eye movements)." "Talks or yells while accomplishing computer interface tasks." "Improves performance over time of tasks required by the program." That one needed a scale, so she could rate where each of her subjects was today, and watch to see if it changed. She decided on a scale of game competence of one to twenty-five, and put her own mark at zero. Richie was about a two, and his mentor, Mark, was a nineteen. Will was the wizard of the arcade; he could get one quarter in Tempest to last longer than Susan had stayed to watch. "Sociability/level of interaction with others on a scale of 1 to 10." Two subcategories there: interaction with other people while playing the same game with them; interaction with other people between games. She labeled the games "programs," though. She wanted to do this project, and she wasn't sure Father would approve it if he knew it was about video games.

Graphs. Columns. Terms. Parameters. The order calmed her; the growing stack of scientific-looking papers on the desk pleased her. As long as she had this to show to Father, she should be all right.

When she finished tallying observations, she picked up Nathan's bone. Holding it, she went to lean against the wall, wondering if it would give her extra power here at home.

She closed her eyes and tuned in to her house.

Silence. No warmth or aliveness, not like Nathan's house. The furnace clicked on. A board creaked. She liked knowing about those things, but it wasn't as though the house were her friend. The house didn't speak in her mind the way Nathan's house had.

Was there a way to change that? A way to wake the house up?

Maybe if it were awake, it would care what was happening inside it. Maybe it could learn to close its own doors. Maybe, somehow, it could help Mother.

She went to her desk, took another sheet of notebook paper, and wrote EXPERIMENT 2 at the top.

For this she needed a code. Or a really good hiding place. This wasn't going to be science as Father understood science. She didn't want him to understand it. He should never see these notes.

She could keep them in her room in the haunted house.

But in the meantime, she could use code. She needed a theory and a method of testing it, but once she had those, she could just write down things like "Attempt 1: 5:15 P.M. Monday October 25, 1982. Result: . . . " Then expand on her notes once she got to safety.

Hypothesis: A house treated like a person could become a person.

Wait. She was coming up with theories without using the resources available to her to check them. How had Nathan's house become so alive?

She could ask it.

# chapter eleven

THE HOUSE GREETED her with music Tuesday afternoon.

She set her school bag on the kitchen floor and leaned against the wall, let the colors and energy from her last game of Centipede fade from her mind. A melody, aching and sad, played somewhere deep in the house. At first she wondered whether she was able to hear the past now. Her house sense opened. She realized Julio was practicing violin.

She stood with her hand on the wall, her eyes closed, awake to the house's sense of itself as a living web of energy. There was the fuzzing of light lines she knew meant living warmth: Julio. Something in the configuration of his image echoed the melody he was playing. She felt as though she could see sound.

There were two other living energy images in the house; she knew before she left the dining room that Edmund was up in the attic, that Deirdre sat on the stairs, waiting for her.

"Can you do furniture?" Deirdre asked as soon as Susan faced her.

"Come with me." Susan set her school bag on the stairs, then led Deirdre into the living room. She stood in front of the fireplace and studied the wall above the mantel. "There was something yesterday I never got a chance to look at." She stroked the bone and requested that the house bring the portrait again.

The woman in the oil painting was very young, her smile fresh and friendly. She sat in a rattan rocker with a broad oval seat back. Her black hair was piled high on her head. She looked cool in her mint-green dress with its scattered embroidery of white vines and flowers, its puffed, elbow-length sleeves, its very full skirt. In one relaxed hand she held a small pocket watch, its cover up so that they could see the design on it: two doves, touching beaks. Her eyes were a vivid blue Susan recognized.

"She's beautiful," Deirdre said.

Susan felt Nathan form behind her. She turned.

"Mother," he said. He looked at Susan for a long moment, then walked past her to stand and stare up at the portrait.

Susan touched Deirdre's shoulder, and they slipped away.

"Can I visit your room?" Deirdre asked when they reached the upstairs sitting room.

"Sure." The door to Susan's room opened without a touch.

"I wish I could do that," Deirdre said. "Just think and make things happen."

"That's not how it works. Really. You guys don't

seem to get this, but I'm not controlling anything. House likes me, and it does things like that to be nice to me. Please have a seat." She waved toward the bed.

Deirdre sat down and stared at her gray-and-blue running shoes. "Susan, did you ever have a girl for a friend before?"

"I don't know," she said, and then, "Oh." She recognized what was happening inside her. There was a point in some conversations—the ones where she had feelings it was better no one, including herself, knew about—at which her mind turned off, and she answered every question with "I don't know." It usually didn't happen this fast.

Why did her mind always go blank when she talked to Deirdre?

Maybe Deirdre asked her hard questions.

She sat on the bed and concentrated until she could remember the question. What was hard about it? "I don't remember having any real friends besides Julio, and maybe his mom," she said. That was the problem: a normal person should have lots of friends. The people she watched stealthily on afternoon TV always seemed to.

Deirdre said, "Well, I never really had a girl for a friend before. I thought Trudie was my friend for a while, but she wasn't. She was just looking for ways to hurt me, and they weren't hard to find. My dad wanted a son. He didn't get one." Deirdre shrugged. "I try to be the next best thing. We do all this stuff together—basketball, fishing, shooting, watching sports on TV together. We only went hunting once. I shot a pigeon, and I swore I'd never do that again." She shuddered. "The blood on the feathers. Its eyes. . . I can't stand hurting animals. So we go target shooting instead. I love the things I do with Dad, but that makes me too weird for the girls I know in school. But it's okay with Julio and Edmund, even though neither of them does much of that kind of stuff. Julio lives with his mom, and Edmund's parents are pacifists and never do anything violent. Anyway, I wondered if I was doing something wrong—I mean, something that would bother any girl I tried to be friends with—or if it's just you. You know what I mean?"

"It's me. I don't talk to people," said Susan.

"But you *have* to talk to people, don't you? You can't keep everything inside. Don't you ever get mad and want the person you're mad at to know?"

"Oh, no," said Susan, her eyes widening.

"Why not?"

"It's dangerous." Susan covered her mouth with both hands.

"How can it be dangerous? My mom and dad and I yell at each other all the time. I know not everybody's like that. At Edmund's, they're so nice it makes you sick. I'm trying to train his little sister to argue. I don't think Julio and his mom have yelling fights. They just have intense discussions. How do you rich people handle it?"

Susan hesitated. "We don't have feelings," she said at last.

"Excuse me for living, but I fell off the hearse," said Deirdre. "Puh-leeze. That's no answer. What do you do when you get mad?"

Susan looked at her lap, picked at the edge of a quilt square on the bedspread. The internal freeze started at the tips of her toes, worked its way through her feet, up her calves, past her knees, up her thighs, and on up her body. She never felt much of what was going on in her body, but when the freeze came, it was as if she had no body at all. If she didn't have a body, Father wouldn't be able to fix or threaten her. He wouldn't own or order her.

Cold was comforting. Quiet. Insulating.

So familiar.

"What? What? Tell me." Deirdre poked her.

Susan let the cold wrap her round.

"Okay." Deirdre shook Susan's arm gently. "I'm sorry. Whatever it is, I'm sorry. But I don't know what it is. What did I do wrong?"

There was a warm spot against her thigh. Susan touched it: a lump in her pocket. Nathan's bone. She tucked her hand into the pocket and gripped the bone, and warmth spread from it up her arm, chasing the chill.

*But I like the cold.*

*It's not helping,* House said.

*Isn't it?*

*Talk to Deirdre, Susan.*

Susan sighed. She turned words over in her mind,

knew she would never have been able to say them at home. But this wasn't home. She said: "How can I talk to you? Every time I say anything, you argue with me."

"But what I say shouldn't hurt you. It's just words."

"You think words don't hurt?"

They stared at each other.

"I guess that was a stupid thing to say," Deirdre said. "I guess if you don't talk much, you probably think words count more. What does your family talk about over supper?"

"Father tells us about his day in court. Mother talks about her clubs or her volunteer work at the hospital. If they run out of things to say, I mention something I learned in school."

"Yuck. Boring! Sounds like a nightmare."

"But it isn't," Susan whispered. "If that's what happens, everything's all right. If it's different, something horrible might happen. That's the nightmare."

"What might happen?"

"No," she whispered. The blank wall rose up in her thoughts, blocked everything. "No, that's not for you. That's inside is all. It's nothing. What did you do in sports today? We played field hockey again."

Deirdre thumped her fists on her thighs. "Don't switch subjects. I want to be your friend. You can tell me things."

"Not these things. No, that's not ready to happen yet. No. There are knives on these words." She tried to breathe, but it was hard. She leaned against the wall, and the house's breathing steadied her.

To be able to talk about it. To let someone else know. To have someone tell her whether this was normal or not.

Maybe someone to tell her whether she could do anything about it.

She clenched her hand around Nathan's bone and stared at Deirdre, who looked back, brown eyes bright under her shaggy brown hair, all her habitual bluster gone. Susan bit her lip. Her stomach twisted, and her throat tightened. She shook her head. "No," she whispered. "No, I can't tell you. I'm sorry." She turned toward the wall, blinking and swallowing.

"It's okay. It's okay." Deirdre touched her hand. She sat quiet, waiting for Susan to compose herself, then said, "Hey. I want to show you something. My room, all right? You have to promise not to tell anybody what I have in there, though. Okay?"

"All right." Susan felt as though she had been stretched and released but couldn't return to her original shape.

Deirdre tugged her to her feet and led her to the master bedroom.

Sitting on the dresser were four dolls. One, the size of a six-month-old baby, had disturbing blue glass eyes set in a porcelain face. It wore a red velvet dress with a lace collar, a ribbon belt, and white kid boots fastened with tiny buttons. One was a raggedy baby doll with the crinkled, dulled hair dolls got from too much loving. The other two were a very ancient, wicked-eyed Barbie and a fuzzy-headed Ken.

Susan stared at them. Confusion immobilized her. This was Deirdre's secret? She never would have guessed.

Deirdre stared at the dolls, too, then touched a finger to Ken's head. She glanced sideways at Susan. "Well." She sighed. "I'm smuggling them in in my backpack. It's my one true vice. I don't understand why, but I collect them. I want them. Once I have them, I love them. It bugs me. It's such a—*a girl* thing to do. I'm too old for it, and I don't even know what to do with them. Why me?"

Susan picked up the glass-eyed porcelain doll. It had long wavy brown hair. Its face looked vacant and spooky.

"That one was my grandmother's, and the Barbie and Ken were my mom's when she was a little girl. The baby is mine. Guess I knew what to do with her when I got her. I dragged her all over the place when I was five and six, and she sure got beat up. Haven't done that in ages, though. Maybe if Mom wasn't allergic to animals, I could have gotten a dog, and I wouldn't be like this." Deirdre fiddled with Barbie's ponytail. "Or maybe I would be anyway. I have more dolls at home. And I go to toy stores and just drool over them. I spend most of my allowance on them. I don't even play with them."

"But you could." Susan picked up Ken and brought him to the bed. She set him on the knobbly white bedspread. "Suppose he's a journeyman wizard, on a voyage

across the land of ice. He's been set a task by the master
wizard which is supposed to teach him one of the keys of
knowledge. Obviously he's wearing a disguise." She
knelt beside the bed, leaned on her elbows and looked at
the doll, which wore an approximation of jeans and a
brown sport shirt. "He should have a familiar." She went
to the bookshelf and selected a crockery dog from the
knickknacks. "Maybe this is a person under an enchant-
ment. You can never judge by appearance in a fairy tale."

"Are you making this up?" said Deirdre.

"Borrowing from stories," Susan said. "I read a lot,
and sometimes I make up stories. I never thought about
using dolls before, though. I have three at home, but
Father bought them for me when I was little, and I was
only supposed to look at them. It never occurred to me
to do anything with them."

"I'd like to see them. Well, now you know my secret."

"Thank you. It's a good one." She pushed herself to
her feet and took Ken and the dog back to the dresser.
"I won't tell anybody."

A knock sounded on the door.

"Who is it and what do you want?" asked Deirdre.

"Edmund. Can I come in?"

Deirdre glanced at the collection on the dresser, then
at Susan. Susan narrowed her eyes. She stroked the
dresser, touched the porcelain knobs of the top drawer.
It opened.

"Ha! I tried to open that. Couldn't get it to budge.
Thought it must have swollen shut." Deirdre placed the

dolls carefully in the drawer and closed it. "All right, you can come in."

Edmund was wearing jeans and a black leather jacket. He carried a green backpack. "I didn't mean to bother you. I just wanted to try some magic, if that's okay with you. If it's okay with the house." He glanced at the ceiling, then at Susan.

Susan and Deirdre looked at each other. "What kind of magic?" Deirdre asked. Susan leaned against the nearest wall, waiting for the house's response.

"It's a sort of—well, I'm making this up as I go along, out of things I find in books. It's an opening thing, to start things right, invite friendly power to come, and to clean out whatever bad things happened here before. I've done this at home, but I couldn't tell whether it worked. Seems like anything could happen here. If it does—" He smiled at them. "Oh, if it does. . . ."

"Do you want us to help?" Deirdre asked.

"Yes. I was hoping you would. I hope Julio and Nathan will help, too."

Susan felt the house's interest. Messages traveled through its walls. She sensed their passage, their communication with Nathan, sensed that he touched the portrait in the living room just before it disappeared, then rose through the ceiling to emerge in Julio's room.

"It's okay," Susan said. "They're coming."

"Can you believe what she just said?" Deirdre asked Edmund. "This is the third time I've come here. I think it's still Saturday morning, but the alarm hasn't gone off yet. I must be dreaming."

"Do you want me to pinch you?" asked Edmund.

"No. I don't want to wake up. This is too cool."

Julio knocked, and he and Nathan came in.

Edmund said, "I don't have a lot of tools or anything, just ideas. Will you guys come upstairs with me?"

Everyone followed him up the attic stairs.

He had cleaned the window and swept the floor, tacked Indian-print bedspreads to the rafters in the ceiling, and sketched a circle about three feet in diameter on the floor with green chalk. A Coleman camping lantern hung from a hook on the ceiling. He switched it on. Blue-green light spilled softly across the floor.

Edmund went to the dresser, opened his backpack, and got out several things: a compass, something rectangular wrapped in a green silk scarf, a bottle of clear liquid, a white saucer, a green votive-sized candle, a book of matches, and a plastic bag with leaves in it. "Ready?"

Susan remembered the long moment she had waited, holding the skull, for the others to step forward and place their hands on it. "What do we do?"

"What are all these things for?" Deirdre stooped beside him.

"I'll explain as I go along. I don't know how well this will work. Never know till you try. Nathan? Julio?"

"Go ahead," said Julio. Nathan nodded.

Edmund consulted his compass, then untied the

green silk scarf to reveal a deck of cards. "These are my tarot cards. I'm going to use them for focus. These are the aces, for making a beginning. Swords are north, wands south, cups west, and pentacles east." He laid the brightly colored cards out around the edge of the circle, one aligned in each direction. "Now, if you each sit in front of a card, we'll have our circle. Deirdre, you're swords."

"Is that because I fight all the time?" She sat down facing the ace of swords.

"No. Well, kind of. The simple way to assign these suits is by hair and eye color. Swords are for people with brown hair and brown eyes. Julio, you're pentacles, for people with black hair and black eyes. Nathan, you don't fit, so you get cups, because Susan is a perfect wand, since they're for people with blonde hair and blue eyes. Cups is my suit. Brown hair, hazel eyes. But I'm in the middle, so I don't have a card."

Edmund sat in the center of the chalk circle, and they settled on the floor around him. Susan looked at her card and felt her stomach clench. A white hand came out of a gray cloud: it held an upraised stick with a few leaves on it. Edmund, facing her, set the green candle on the white saucer and placed it before her. "Your sign is fire," he said. "Nathan is water, Deirdre's air, Julio's earth, so together, we represent everything."

"How is my sign fire?" Susan asked. Her voice came out too high. "My sign is a stick."

"The fire is locked inside the wand. It's power that

can come out at your command, if you have matches."
He studied her face. "Imagine that wand burning up,
Susan," he said, "but wait just a minute before you do."

"How come a pentacle stands for earth?" Julio
asked.

Edmund shook his head. "I haven't been able to figure that out. Sometimes they stand for money—metal—
that's from the earth. Lots of times the pentacle cards
show gardens, sometimes people working the earth. Also,
I'm not sure why swords stand for air. Cups make sense
to me for water, though, because they can hold it. Also a
lot of the cups cards have water in the background. But
then a bunch of the others do, too. I'm still studying."

He opened the bottle. "This is salt water. Salt is of
the earth, and purifies. Water cleanses." He took some
of the leaves out of the plastic bag. "This is marjoram.
Somebody told me it was a good herb." He laid the
leaves before him, and took a deep breath, then let it
out. "All right. Now we cast the circle. Hold hands with
each other."

Edmund glanced at Nathan, who looked down at his
own hands. Susan held out her left hand to him, with
his bone still in her palm. He took her hand, then
reached to Deirdre, who hesitated, then clasped hands.
"Yikes," she squeaked.

Edmund glanced back at her over his shoulder. "You
okay?"

"His hand is still freezing. How come I can touch
you, Nate?"

"Maybe because I'm touching the bone at the same time? And Susan's touching it and me?"

Deirdre's shoulders heaved in an exaggerated shudder, but she didn't let go.

Julio reached for Susan's and Deirdre's hands. Susan closed her eyes, disturbed by the contrast between the freezing hand in her left and the warm hand in her right. Under and around her, she sensed the house's energy, its breath and pulse. Presently, Nathan's hand grew warmer; she sensed the house putting more energy into him.

"Breathe with me," said Edmund. His voice was quiet and low. "Imagine you can feel energy coming up from the earth. It goes in and out with your breath."

Susan opened her eyes and watched the movement of his chest as he breathed. She matched breaths with Edmund, and sensed Julio doing it, too. The house synchronized with them, and through the house, Nathan did, even though he didn't really breathe. For a moment, she heard Deirdre's breathing because it didn't match. Then it joined the rhythm.

"We are one creature, breathing together. Power comes into us from the earth, from the air. It goes clockwise around the circle. Let it pass through you. Feel its motion."

Susan felt a tingling that reminded her of the way House had tingled at her through Nathan's bone. Energy traveled from Julio's hand up her arm, across her back, along her other arm, and into Nathan's hand in an unending circuit. The feeling grew stronger.

Edmund lit the candle. "Hail, powers of earth and east," he said, facing Julio. He turned to Susan. "Hail, powers of fire and south." Then to Nathan. "Hail, powers of water and west." He turned to face Deirdre. "Hail, powers of air and north. We salute you with water and salt." He sprinkled drops in all four directions. "We salute you with fire and air." He held the candle toward each of them. "Powers, strengthen our circle."

Through her house sense, Susan could almost see the energy as it traveled, a gray-blue spinning funnel, wide as their arms at the base, narrowing near the top. It reminded her of the spiraled fossil in her sea stone. Edmund sat calm in the center of it, his spine straight, his breathing even.

"Look at your cards, and let your particular energy flow through you to become part of our circle," said Edmund.

Susan felt half asleep. She concentrated on the card before her, thinking of the wand as one of the things Father used to beat Mother: power invoked and misused. She called to the fire to burn the wand, make it so hot Father could no longer hold it. She imagined the wand bursting into flames. Waves of energy swept through her, entered her right hand, departed through her left, and each wave seemed stronger.

"We are gathering energy," Edmund said. "When I say the word, we will send it out. May this energy make this space safe for all of us, according to free will, and for the good of all." He waited a moment, then said, "Now!"

Susan felt the energy whoosh up in a cone, draw to a point somewhere above them but below the ceiling, then spread to seep into House, which felt surprised, then puzzled but intrigued.

Edmund licked his lips. His voice was a little hoarse as he said, "Thanks to everything that came together. Thanks for coming. Thanks for working through us. Thanks for leaving us. We thank you and release you. So let it be.

"Everyone, relax. Lie down if you want. Let the rest of the power flow out of you, back into earth and air, fire and water." Edmund crushed the leaves of marjoram, spicing the air with its scent.

Deirdre collapsed. "Is it over? Boy, was that ever weird."

"You felt something happen, right?" asked Edmund. He lifted the candle and blew it out.

"Are you kidding? Didn't you feel it? I felt like I was in a washing machine, going around and around and. . ."

Julio yawned into the back of his hand.

"Nathan?" Edmund said.

"It worked. I don't know what it did, but something happened."

"I felt it," said Edmund. "It was like being in a cathedral, sort of, the arches way up high, and light coming in through stained glass. Only this time I felt like I could—could guide it." His eyes had gone very green. "Sort of scary. What if I did it wrong? Susan, are you all right?"

Her eyes dropped before his gaze. She glanced at her watch.

"Susan?"

"All right."

Edmund gathered the cards together and traced a figure on each one before he stowed them with the rest of the deck in the green scarf.

"Is that magic?" Deirdre said from the floor. "It wasn't like—twitching your nose and turning somebody into something, or waving a wand and making a pumpkin into a carriage. I didn't see anything happen, but it was a lot of work, and now I'm totally zonked."

"I think that's how magic works," said Edmund.

"When Susan does things, it's not like that," Deirdre said in a sleepy voice. "The doors just open. Things appear. She doesn't get tired by it."

"But I don't do magic," said Susan. She tried to focus on her watch. Tiredness swamped her. "House makes all the effort. All I do is—ask it."

"Huh. Words," Deirdre murmured. "Word Magic."

# chapter twelve

SUSAN STARED AT rows and rows of bright-colored pictures of vegetables in the canned food aisle of the supermarket: orange carrots, green beans, purple beets, yellow corn, with lines of silver shining at the tops and bottoms of the cans. She let her eyes unfocus until the colors blurred with kaleidoscopic pleasantness. Supermarket air, a mixture of scents from produce and bakery, dairy, raw meat, detergent, refrigerator coolant. She sniffed it, noticed that the metal of the shopping cart handle had warmed under her right hand; the bone in her left hand was body temperature, a strange shape, yet not separate from her.

She loved grocery shopping with Juanita on Wednesdays.

"I know you," said a voice behind her.

Susan's hand tightened on the cart handle. Juanita, ahead of her in the aisle, chose a can of chile peppers, then glanced at Susan.

"Yeah, you," said the voice. "Turn around. You were that girl playing tricks on me at the house on Lee Street."

Susan turned to face Trudie. She raised her eyebrows in imitation of Mother's Imperial Manner. "I'm afraid you have me confused with somebody else," she said.

"Oh, no, I don't." Trudie glared at her. "I should call the cops and tell them about you and your friends trespassing up there."

Susan yawned into the back of her hand. "You're free to do whatever you like. I'm sure it doesn't concern me."

"We'll see about that," said Trudie, with a dark smile. She stalked away, assurance in every line of her body.

"Susana?" Juanita said. "You been going to that house?"

Susan looked at her. Every Wednesday, she and Juanita took the coupon supplements from the weekly paper and went shopping. Father felt shopping was a survival skill a woman needed, and Juanita hadn't argued with him.

"I know Julio goes there," said Juanita. "He always tells me where he is. He doesn't tattle on his friends, though. You been going up there?"

Susan bit her lip. "After school. We have permission."

"What if that girl goes to the police? Will you get in trouble?"

Susan looked down at her hands. "I don't know. Maybe if we're prepared—" She thought about House's defense systems. She smiled.

"I've heard stories about that house," said Juanita.

"An *ánima*, a ghost. Screams. Shapes in the window, the death of a child, and the *sombras*, shadows hanging around the house. Besides, it's very old. Is it safe, Susana?"

"The construction is sound."

"You didn't answer my question." Juanita pulled the cart along the aisle, paused to check their list against the sale prices. She glanced back at Susan.

"It's safer than being home alone after school. Julio's there, after all."

Juanita raised her eyebrows, then took four cans of green beans from a shelf and stacked them in the cart. "Well, listen. If things go bad, if the police get you or something like that, call me, all right? Don't you go calling your father. Call me at the Grants' if I'm not working at your place."

"Oh, Juanita." Susan darted around the cart and hugged her.

There was so much they had never talked about. Susan wasn't sure what Juanita knew about what Father did to Mother. How could she clean up afterward and not know? What could she do if she did know? Anything more than Susan could? She was an adult. She didn't live at the house. But Father knew how to ruin people, even people who didn't live with him.

Like Mother, Juanita would protect Susan from Father if she could. Susan hadn't known that before.

❧

Thursday afternoon, after a brief visit to the video

arcade during which she asked quick questions of her informants and only played two games herself, she met Nathan in the brambles as she sneaked around House. "I'm all the way out," he said.

She gripped the bone. "Does this mean you can go anywhere you like? Could you come to the beach with me?"

"I don't know yet. I haven't gone very far. Just to stand under the sky during the day . . . " He looked up and smiled at the overcast sky, his eyes translucent in the gray light. "Oh, Susan."

"It seems like anything can happen," she said, catching a little of his joy. Then she remembered. "Oh, no. Anything *can* happen—"

Edmund, Deirdre, and Julio came through the blackberry bushes. "Can you believe they made everybody stay after school for *that*?" Deirdre asked. "That dumb lecture. It was so lame! What a waste of time."

"Quit complaining. It's over, and we're here now," said Edmund.

"Quiet!" Susan said.

The three of them checked, looked at Susan and Nathan. Edmund blinked. He glanced from Susan to Nathan. Nathan smiled at him.

"What do you mean, quiet?" Deirdre demanded.

Susan frowned. "We have to be more careful! Yesterday, I saw that girl, Trudie, at the market. She said she'd tell the police we were trespassing. What if she told them? What if they're watching?"

Julio glanced back over his shoulder. They stood motionless, their breaths the only sound. Then they ran for the back door, which opened wide as they crossed the porch.

As soon as they were inside, the door closed itself.

"Where do we hide?" Edmund asked.

"That secret panel?" asked Deirdre.

Susan let her house awareness open. "There's an entrance from your room, too, Deirdre," she said. "There's this place—you can't stand up in it, but it's like a little room."

"The crawl space over the kitchen," said Nathan. "Then there's the housekeeper's secret stairs. House could close the doors at either end and make them stick. There's enough room in there for all of you."

"And there's the basement," said Susan.

"Where are all these places? We haven't even explored the house," Edmund said.

"You haven't looked in the front parlor. You haven't seen half the attic," Nathan said. "Your room is only the finished part. There's a panel in back of the dresser that leads to the unfinished half, where Papa stored all the broken furniture and worn-out things."

Footsteps sounded on the back porch. "Hey!" yelled a man's voice.

They ran through the house and up the stairs. The master bedroom door opened for them, and they rushed inside. The secret panel popped open, too.

"Anybody bring a flashlight?" Deirdre asked.

"Just get in!" Julio pushed her forward, and they all stooped and crawled in.

The ceiling started about four and a half feet above the floor, and sloped down from there. The roof trusses were visible, but the floor looked finished and had a braided rag rug on it.

They only had a second to see details before the panel shut, leaving them in absolute darkness.

Nobody spoke or moved.

Below them, a cascade of knocks sounded.

The crawl space was almost over the back porch, and it wasn't insulated.

"Hey! You kids! I know you're in there! I saw you go in! I can hear you moving around up there!"

Susan huddled against the wall and listened to the harsh breathing in the dark around her. Someone slid a foot sideways. The darkness felt thick and collapsing.

"Hey, you in there! Open this door. This is the police. You were observed entering the premises." The yell came right up through the floor, and when he knocked on the door and rattled the knob, they felt the impacts.

Susan held her breath. In the silence that followed, she didn't hear anyone else breathe either.

"This place is off limits to everybody. It's old and dangerous! You could fall through the floor and hurt yourself. You shouldn't be hanging around in here. Come out!" He pounded on the door. "Do I need to get an ax?"

They heard his startled cry as the door opened and he fell inside. "All right. Who did that? Where did you run away to?"

"Huh," Julio whispered. "There's something—"

Footsteps sounded directly beneath them. He went through the kitchen and beyond, into the dining room. "Now he's checking the front parlor," whispered Susan. "Now the living room."

As he moved toward the front of the house, the sound of his progress faded.

Edmund pulled a flashlight from his pack. He switched it on and shone light around the crawl space. The rug appeared in the circle of light, the boards of the ceiling, and then, chalk-white bones and tatters.

Deirdre let out a shriek, then clapped her hand over her mouth. "What's that?" she whispered.

"It's only Nathan," whispered Susan.

"Yikes! What's he doing in here?"

"We haven't figured that out yet. Nathan doesn't remember. But you don't have to be scared, Dee. You've already met him."

"Nathan? Nathan, are you in here?"

"Yes, I'm here." He sat against the wall beside Susan.

Deirdre grabbed Edmund's hand and directed the flashlight beam toward Nathan. He shielded his eyes from the light. "Are you sure you don't want us to bury you? That's a heck of a thing to keep around the house."

"It should stay here for now. And remember, if you bump into it in the dark, there's one just like it inside you."

"Oh! Ewww!" She released Edmund's hand and felt the bones in her own wrist. "That's a horrible idea."

Edmund switched off the light. "Is there any ventilation in here?"

Susan let her house sense open again, and no longer felt trapped in a small airless space. Air flowed around them from small vents above. Susan knew that the invader would be kept below, not allowed up here. "Yes," she whispered.

"Why'd you turn off the light?" Deirdre asked Edmund.

"I want to save it for when we need it. I don't think we'll be moving much right now. Are you okay in the dark, Deirdre?"

"Will you hold my hand?" Her whisper was very thin.

"Sure."

Susan felt Nathan vanish from the crawl space, felt his energy move to the living room. She bit her lip.

The low moans that had greeted them when they first entered the house began. The sounds started softly, then rose. Susan's chest tightened. Intolerable sadness twisted her heart.

She reached out in the dark and put her hand firmly around Julio's ankle. He jumped. "Don't do that!" he whispered.

"Shut up."

"I can't take this," cried the intruder. "I cannot take this!" He ran from the house.

Beneath them, the back door slammed shut.

The panel in Deirdre's room slid open. Dazzling daylight poured in.

"Thanks, House," Edmund said.

"Yeah, thanks," said Deirdre. She let go his hand and scooted out of the crawl space.

Susan released Julio's ankle and rubbed her eyes. When she followed Julio out into the open, Nathan was there already.

Susan went to him. In his moans, she heard the pain of someone trapped and alone forever, someone who had lost every friend he had ever made. "It hurts so much."

"It's just an act."

"I don't believe you."

"Believe me. You're all here now, and it's just an act."

She sniffled and looked away from him. Julio approached. "Who was that?" he asked.

"A policeman," said Nathan. "Officer Hawkins."

"Hawkins?" Julio said. "Wait a minute—"

"How'd you find out?" asked Deirdre.

"He had a name tag. Now that I've got my freedom, I can follow him and see where he goes. Excuse me." He vanished.

"His freedom?" Edmund asked.

Susan looked at the bone in her hand. "He couldn't leave House. For sixty-three years, he hasn't been able to leave House, except on Halloween. But now, he can get outside. That was our experiment. I take this bone out of House, and he can go out, too."

"So if we took the whole skeleton away—" said Deirdre.

"Who knows what would happen," Julio finished. "Forget that, Deirdre, unless that's what he wants. This is really weird, but we're lucky to have him. We can't mess this up just because you're scared of some old bones."

Nathan reappeared. "He's coming back."

# chapter thirteen

AGAIN, THEY HUDDLED in the low-ceilinged darkness. Their breaths crowded them. Susan smelled Deirdre's plastic slicker and her own damp wool coat and some-body's tennis shoes. She clutched Julio's hand this time instead of his ankle. In her other hand, she held Nathan's bone. Chill flowed from beside her, where he sat.

"I can't let myself be chased off by some dumb sound effects," the man muttered below them. "I tell anybody that and my name is mud. Sound effects. Implies a sound system. Somebody's making mischief. Besides, I saw those kids go inside. This place doesn't look safe. I have to get them out of here. Where are they?"

He passed beneath them again and went farther into the house. "Kids? I don't want to hurt you. I just want to get you out of here," he called. "Come on."

"Maybe we should just go down," Edmund whis-pered. "Let him lead us away, and then sneak back."

"What if he's lying?" asked Deirdre.

A doorknob rattled below. A door slammed open, and

126

thuds followed, accompanied by a yell of surprise. A
door slammed shut.

"What?" Deirdre said.

Susan leaned her head against the wall and opened
her house sense. "He fell down the basement stairs,"
she said.

"Help!" called the stranger's voice, muffled by walls
and floors and ceilings. "Somebody?"

Susan reported, "House closed the door on him. He's
down there in the dark."

"So we can leave now?" asked Deirdre.

"You kids?" called the man. "Hey?"

"Susan, I want to get out now, please," Deirdre said.
She crept to the secret panel.

Susan released Julio's hand and folded her arms
across her chest. She held the bone tight and called on
her house sense, requesting that the secret panel open.
A long minute ticked past, and the panel opened.

"Thank you." Deirdre scrambled out into the daylit
bedroom.

"We have to go downstairs," Julio said. "We can't just
leave him down there. Besides, if his name's Hawkins, he
might be somebody I know. There's a Jeff Hawkins whose
grandmother lives next door to me. I think he's a cop."

"But that means he knows who you are and where
you live. Now's our chance to get away without him
catching us," said Deirdre. "The house will open the
door for him as soon as we're gone, right, Nathan?"

"I don't know," said Nathan. He sounded upset.

"I'll let him out," said Julio. "I've got the least to lose. My mother already knows I'm here." He went to the door. When he turned the knob and the door didn't open, he glanced at Susan. She nodded, held the bone, and addressed House. The door refused to cooperate. She went to it. It opened when she turned the knob.

She sighed. "I guess I'll go too." Hopelessness overwhelmed her. She would help, and they would arrest her, and Father would discover that she wasn't going home after doing her research at the arcade. What kind of penalty would Mother suffer for that? Every time Mother suffered, Susan felt sick, too. Her stomach hurt, even if she could get every other part of her to freeze out of her awareness. She threw up, and she had to keep that quiet, too, or Father got even more upset. She couldn't stand that Mother was punished for anything Susan did. She couldn't stand it, and it happened anyway, and there was nothing she could do to stop it but try to never get caught doing anything wrong. She felt sick as she started down the stairs.

Time slowed and stopped. She felt the banister under her fingers, its surface polished from generations of use. Beneath her feet, she sensed the gentle slope in the center of the stair, where the wood had worn down; the air was rich with the scent of the sea.

*Will such terrible things happen to you if you stay to open the door for this man?* House asked.

*Yes.*

*I thought maybe he could protect you. I know you're*

*frightened. When you did Edmund's ritual inside me, I felt your fears. I know you need more help than I can give you. I thought—*

An image of her mother took color and light inside her head. Mother hid her head under a pillow, as if that could make the world and her own bruised and damaged body go away. Mother did not have Susan's ability to ignore physical hurt. She wept and suffered, and finally, when Father had left the house again, she went to one of her secret places where a bottle was, and drank a tunnel away from the pain.

*This will happen,* Susan thought, *if this man finds me here.*

*I understand.*

Time shifted into present again, and she turned to look up the stairs. Julio, Edmund's flashlight in his hand, was right behind her.

"The basement door will open for you," she told him. She glanced at her watch, then went to her room. The door slammed shut behind her. She collapsed onto the bed and buried her face in the pillow, breathing its old-trunk smell.

❧

A touch on her shoulder roused her from an exhausted half-sleep. She turned over, discovered Nathan beside the bed, rubbed her sandy eyes, and looked at her watch. "Oh, no!" It was already after five. How could she have fallen asleep? She hadn't written up today's notes, either. "What happened?" She sat up. She had to get home fast and change. She would need every shortcut she could find.

He helped her to her feet and, holding her hand, he picked her school bag up. "Julio went downstairs. He let the policeman out. Julio said he heard shouts as he happened to walk by. I don't think the man believed him. Susan, I don't know what's going on. House doesn't do things like this."

"It's trying to help me. Was the man all right?"

"He was fine. Julio left with him. Then Deirdre and Edmund got away. They tried to wake you before they left. They can't walk through walls, though, and the door refused to open."

"I've got to get home. I'm not sure I can come back tomorrow. I'd better be careful. But remember our date on Halloween, okay? Sunday night? You're coming to my house, right?" She felt strange asking for it, but she thought: *I've never been anywhere or seen anyone on Halloween. I want this more than I want anything else.*

"I won't forget," Nathan said.

Susan ran all the way home.

# chapter fourteen

"YOU HAVE SUCH beautiful hands," said Mother. She applied a second coat of clear polish to Susan's nails. Susan felt the brush touch the skin, a cool flicker, like a snowflake just before it melted.

The light in the kitchen was muted; the fluorescent strips under the cabinets were on, and the round lantern over the kitchen table, but the brushed chrome refrigerator looked dark gray, and the gold and white figurings in the linoleum were subdued. Susan had scraped and stacked the dishes from dinner; the air smelled faintly of shepherd's pie and strongly of nail polish.

Susan studied the crown of her mother's head. Mother had honey-blonde hair, a darker shade than Susan's; it had a lacquered look, a perfect sweep forward. Susan wanted to touch it—but they never touched, except in the framework of an activity like a manicure.

"What are you doing these days?" Mother asked. She released Susan's hand. "Blow on those, but not too hard."

"Oh, I . . ."

"Do you have lots of friends? Are you popular?" Mother stared into Susan's face with hungry eyes.

"I have friends," said Susan. She blew on her fingertips.

"There are so many things about your life that I don't know," said Mother. "Susan, are you happy?"

She was happy when she wasn't home. At home, she was mostly miserable. Which answer would make her mother feel best? Yes, and let it go? Or no, and open up something they never talked about? "I'm happy," she said.

"Tell me true: cross your heart." Mother sketched a cross in the air in front of her pale silk shirt. Susan had never seen her make such a move before, so at odds with her polished appearance. "That took too long for you to say."

Susan thought of Word Magic: of asking House for things, and receiving what she asked for; of Deirdre telling her that friends were for telling things.

"I am happy, in lots of ways, Mother, but there's this thing. . . ." No. She couldn't bring it up. Her stomach already hurt.

"What is it?" Mother glanced toward the kitchen door. She listened, and Susan listened, too. "I think your father's in his study."

"Yes." Susan wondered if Mother had house sense, too. Why didn't she run away from Father if she could tell when he was coming?

Susan's voice dropped to a whisper. "Mother, why do you let him do it to you?"

Mother took Susan's other hand. She got a tool out of her manicure kit and pushed back Susan's cuticles. "I love you, sweetie."

"Mother."

"I love you so much." She stopped working on Susan's fingers and put her hand over her eyes. Then she got a cigarette out of her handbag and lit it. "Your father is a good man, honey," she said. "He works hard. He made this beautiful place for us, and he gives us so much. I'm so stupid about things. I hadn't learned anything when we got married. . . . I was such a child. I couldn't boil water or scrub a floor. I just knew how to be beautiful. He saw great things in me. He was a struggling law student, and I was coasting along in my sorority, going to parties. He told me I could be better than that, that together we could be great." She took a long draw on her cigarette, then blew out the smoke and watched it rise. It looked blue in the muted light. "Look where we are now," she said, her eyes still on the ceiling. "We have so many beautiful things, and a housekeeper to keep them pretty. I have everything I ever wanted when I was a girl." She touched the strand of champagne-colored pearls at her throat.

"But Mother. Why do you let him?" It came out in a whisper.

"He has these tensions at work. He gets so frustrated when he loses a case and some criminal goes free. All these things build up inside him."

Susan studied her hands. The nails on the left were

shiny with fresh polish, and the nails on the right were dull.

"You're the thing he loves most in all the world, Susan. You're our one good and perfect thing. But there are times . . . Sometimes he just . . ." Mother crossed her arms over her stomach and hugged herself, as if her stomach hurt, too. "There are so many things I can't do, Susan. I was never good at diapers or washing up or feeding you, or any of those—those *real* things. There's nothing I can teach you, except grooming, that will get you anywhere. But I can give you this."

Susan wanted to touch her. She wanted to scream or cry.

But she never cried.

Mother stubbed out her cigarette and lifted Susan's right hand, turned it over to study the palm.

❧❦❧

It felt strange to head up Shannon Hill right after school on Friday. Susan's feet wanted to go toward Lee Street. She hadn't yet asked House how it came alive; she hadn't started her second experiment. But she was still disturbed about House and "protectors." So she skipped her visits to the arcade and to the haunted house, and headed home.

When she opened the front door, she sensed movement somewhere in the house. She paused, her hand on the doorknob, and listened.

"Susana? That you? I'm just putting things back in the fridge," Juanita called from the kitchen.

"It's me," Susan yelled. She closed the door and headed toward the kitchen, leaving her school bag on the stairs.

"Want some lemonade? It's probably warm—I just finished defrosting," Juanita said as Susan came in through the swinging door between the dining room and kitchen.

"No, thank you."

"We had somebody over to dinner last night," said Juanita. "So that girl in the supermarket, she told the police, eh? Julio brought one home."

"One what?"

"*Jefe.*" Juanita smiled briefly. "Jeff. He's not a *jefe*, a chief, he's just a boy, really. I watched that one grow up. He's been in and out of my apartment building for years. His *abuela* lives next door to us—she gave Julio his first piano lessons. Jeff is good to his grandmother, and he seems very nice. He and Julio argued, but Jeff didn't arrest Julio. He's just worried. That house, is it safe? You're not going to fall through the floor, are you?"

Susan remembered all she knew about House's structure. "It looks rickety, but it's really not. It's strong."

Juanita put the milk into the refrigerator door and turned the cold back on. "You're sure?"

"Yes."

"Well, you be careful going in and out. People are watching."

# chapter fifteen

TRICK-OR-TREATERS never climbed up Shannon Hill to the Backstrom house. The climb was too steep, and the houses too far apart, making Halloween too much like work.

A full moon shone through breaks in the restless clouds, revealing the emptiness of Nautilus Road. Wind made ocean noises in the trees, casting pine needles, leaves, and occasional branches across the wet asphalt. The air smelled of salt and autumn, rain and rot.

Susan watched the wild, empty Sunday night, then let the ruffled curtain fall back across the window. A narrow crack under the sill let in a teasing breeze that lifted the drapes, then dropped them, sneaking the scent of sea into the room.

She sat at her desk and studied her outline for an extra-credit Constitution paper for her social studies class. Father had assigned her outside reading on the Amendments and the Bill of Rights, and she had gotten absorbed in spite of herself. But tonight she felt too restless to concentrate on it. She sharpened another pencil.

She looked through her notes. She was miles away from a first draft, let alone something she was ready to type. She straightened the edges of her stack of lined paper, then went to the window again.

The curtain twitched out of her fingers. She glanced toward her desk lamp, and saw Nathan's silhouette in profile.

"Did you think I'd come up the road?" he asked, and smiled.

The wind and clouds dumped a brief rage of rain on the roof.

She held out her hands, and he put his in hers. His hands felt warm. "Oh, Nathan," she whispered.

"This one night a year," he said. "Freedom. Freedom to do anything. Come with me, Susan."

She stood a moment, holding his hands, listening to her house. She had heard Father enter his study earlier, and Mother was in her bedroom, two closets away from Susan's room, probably asleep.

"Walk through walls with me," Nathan whispered. "Walk the air. Let the rain fall through you. Let the wind carry you."

"But Mother—if Father comes up and I'm not here—"

His hands tightened on hers. Then he said, "Leave your shadow here. The outside edge, the part that catches light. If you trust me, let me pull your inside out."

The wind called like the sea, and salt soaked the air.

Her blood pulled toward the moon. Yet the shackles of everyday weighed her down, chained her to Earth. In the outer limits of the light, she could almost see them. She gave a low cry. "Oh, yes," she said. "Please. One night. Like you."

"Pose the shadow the way you wish her to appear," he said.

She looked down at her arms, conscious of each golden hair lying against the skin. The shadow! She drew her hands out of his and went to the desk, uncertain of what he wanted. Uncertain, suddenly, of the outcome: if she left her appearance behind, would he like her any longer? Would there be anything left of her?

She gathered her skirt and sat down at her desk, then huddled over her papers. She picked up a sharp pencil and placed her hand, ready to write, at the top of a blank page. Did movie stars feel like this before somebody said "action"? She couldn't suppress a smile.

Nathan touched her forehead, the top of her head, and several places along her spine. "You can come out now," he said, and she lifted her head to look at him, certain it was a joke. A strange sensation in her face, head and neck, like walking through a thin sheet of wind-carried sand. She rose, prickling all over. She felt scrubbed clean.

Susan still sat at the desk. Her hand moved. She bit her eraser, then wrote.

Susan watched Susan, then looked down at her

arms, and saw—nothing. "Am I naked? Am I here at all?" She felt a rush of panic. She wondered if he could even hear her.

"You're here," said Nathan.

"Can you see me? I can't see me."

"I can see you." And she could see his grin.

"What do I look like?"

"For once, don't worry about that. Here." He reached out, and she felt his hand close around hers. "Come."

They went through the wall, and she felt something built into the very structure of the house: a hate, a strength, a rigidity like a tightly clenched fist; and deep underneath, a tiny and very young sadness.

But the next moment, she forgot. Wind lifted them, and its strength and willfulness felt as Susan had always imagined the ocean would feel if she were floating on its surface during a storm, miles from land. Its resistless rise and surge carried them away.

Leaves rose toward them, then dropped earthward. Clouds fled and broke above, letting the moon through. Susan felt moonlight like a skin.

Nothing tied her to Earth.

Below them Guthrie spread out, an ordered grid of streets lying between ocean and lake, lighted by yellow porch lights, orange streetlights, white headlights, red taillights.

Dark figures blew in and out of the circles of light.

"Look! Look! Trick-or-treating!" Susan cried, as

they flew over the pale lace where beaches met foaming waves. They sped out to sea.

"Yes. We didn't do that when I was growing up, but I've watched it from year to year."

"I've only seen it in movies and on TV, never for real."

"Do you want to go back? We can go anywhere."

"Can we fight the wind?"

He pulled her up, through the clouds. She encompassed rain, watched it form and fall, from dark to dark. It hissed into the sea. Then they flew above clouds burnt and shadowed by moonlight.

Stars gemmed the expanse of night sky. The air tasted cool and clean and salt. Another wind caught them and carried them back the way they had come. Susan savored every moment, feeling she would have to store up enough memories tonight to last her the rest of her life. If only she could count on one night a year . . .

She did not feel the cold, but the wind swept across her, sometimes faster than they flew, sometimes slower, and she felt the moisture in the air and tasted its freshness. This invisible self did not feel like the shadow Susan they had left behind. Its arms and legs felt stronger, and when she touched her head, her hair was short and thick.

Nathan pulled them out of the stream of wind and down again through the clouds. The Earth plunged up toward them, and Susan breathed in the speed, thirsty for more. Nathan glanced toward her and did not slow them at all: they hurtled down into the Earth, an instant, total darkness, a tighter atmosphere, but not impassable. She sensed the different textures of earth, stone, pipes and underground wires, tunnels and sewers and underground water. They slowed. Nathan pushed off bedrock and they swam to the surface.

"Oh, wonderful," Susan said. She hugged him, and they laughed, letting earth be solid under them again.

They were standing in a field across from the shopping center. Earth-moving machines loomed large in the half-light; this lot was being made over in the service of more stores. "Come on." Nathan pulled her toward the row of sheltered shops across the street. "I want to show you something."

Few cars were parked under the orange glow from the streetlights. Nathan and Susan scudded across the parking lot like fallen leaves. In the window of a darkened diet center, a mirror captured the orange and dark night. "Shouldn't YOU work on a NEW YOU?" a sign above the mirror read.

She could see Nathan's image in the mirror, his daytime self: shock of dark hair, white shirt lopped in thirds by the black lines of his suspenders, knickers, black stockings, and ankle-high boots. He looked a sturdier and more solid fourteen than she had seen before, his face young but firm and strong. His eyes glowed with blue fire.

She stood beside him, his hand tight in hers; yet nothing stood beside him.

"There is a ritual about this," he said. "If you give your consent, I can make you visible."

"Yes," she said, afraid and curious.

"No, not yet. Informed consent, Susan. If you repeat these words after me, your soul is mine completely until dawn. I can do whatever I like with you."

"Are you going to hurt me?"

"I don't want to, but I don't know what will hurt you. If you see yourself, perhaps you'll understand. In this form, what you look like is a reflection of what you think you are. Will you take this chance?"

A scatter of rain swept the roof of the covered walkway. Susan hugged herself and thought, Why not? Why not choose, for a change, the person who had power over her? Nathan was her friend. "Yes," she said.

He took her hand again and asked her to repeat some words. The ceremony was short, and in a language she had never heard before. At its conclusion, she felt a shudder pass through her.

"Now," he said, "you can see yourself."

She gasped.

It was a slender, sexless thing, with skin of polished steel, catching and casting shimmers of light. Its hair was short, gold-touched platinum, and its eyes were tilted almonds of lapis lazuli with silver flecks. She reached toward the image and it reached toward her, with a long-fingered, nail-less hand.

"Did that hurt?" Nathan asked after a moment.

"How is that thing me?" she asked, watching its lips form her words.

"This is your inner skin, Susan. Armor. It keeps you alive. It keeps you alone. Does it hurt?"

"No," she said. She touched her left forearm with her right hand. She felt the touch; it was like water sliding off a leaf.

"Sometimes parts of it get thinner. Things do get through." He touched her cheek, and she watched, startled, as her cheek turned pink for a second, then steeled over again. "Sometimes the wrong things. But sometimes the right things. Come on. Let's go look at trick-or-treaters."

"But—can they see me?" She pointed to her mirror image.

"It's Halloween," he said. "They won't know they're seeing you with your skin off."

They blew down the street toward houses. They watched a group of sheeted ghosts and plastic-masked witches and goblins run to a front stoop, ring a doorbell, hold bags open for treats, then dash back to rejoin two normally dressed adults who had waited in the shadows. "Milky Ways," said a small goblin.

"Great," said one of the grown-ups. The cluster of creatures moved on.

"What," said Nathan, "is a Milky Way?"

"It's a candy bar. Come on." Susan tugged him up the concrete walk to the lighted front stoop. She rang the doorbell.

"Oh, my," said the girl who answered. It was Pam, from Heron. "That's the best costume I've seen all night. You must have spent ages making it! Or can you buy something like that?"

"No, you can't buy it," Susan said.

"Susan? Is that you? I got stuck on door duty while the little kids are doing the neighborhood. The folks had a party to go to tonight. Who's your friend?"

"Pam, this is Nathan. Nathan, Pam."

Pam held out her hand, and Nathan shook it. "Pleased to meet you," Pam said.

"I am, too. May I have a Milky Way?"

"Oh, you didn't say trick or treat! I lost track. Aren't you guys a little old for this? I figured you were going to Brooks's big party or something."

"Neither of us has ever trick-or-treated before," Susan said.

"Really? You missed all those years of free candy and stomachaches? Well, here." She held out a bowl full of mini candy bars. "Help yourself."

Susan took one, and grinned. Her first trick or treat. Should she keep it? Oh, why get sentimental about a candy bar?

Nathan took one, too. "Thank you."

"You're welcome. Where do you go to school, Nathan?"

"I graduated a long time ago."

"Coulda fooled me. Well, have fun, you guys. See you tomorrow at school, Susan."

"Yes. Thanks. Good night, Pam."

Pam shut the door, and Susan and Nathan went back out to the street.

Nathan unwrapped his candy bar and tried a bite. "Chocolate tastes completely different from the way it used to."

"Do you like it?"

"I think so . . . this is the only night of the year when I have taste and smell, so it's hard to compare. The memories are so old."

They went up some streets and down others, watching phantoms, children dressed in foreign selves. Then, as they passed through a rim of light, somebody said, "Nathan!"

They turned and faced a pirate with an eye patch, a scarf tied around her head, and a wooden cutlass, a tall wizard with a pointy hat, dark shirt and pants and boots, and a black cape decorated with glitter moons and stars, and Julio, wearing an orange choir robe.

"What are you supposed to be?" Nathan asked Julio.

"I haven't figured that out," he said. "I've worn this for the past three years. Got it cheap at a yard sale. Figured it has something to do with music. I would have dressed up as a musician, but even if I could find a good picture of, say, Django Reinhardt or George Gershwin, nobody would know who I was pretending to be." He shrugged.

Deirdre the pirate said, "We force him to come with us. He says he's too old for dress-up. I know it's weird, but when else do Edmund and I get a chance to be our secret selves? Hey, who's your friend? I didn't know you could leave the house."

"I can on Halloween. This is Susan."

"Where's the rest of you?" Deirdre asked, coming closer. For one teetery moment Susan thought Deirdre understood everything that had happened. Then she realized: when Susan was her normal self, she was two inches taller than Deirdre. Somehow her silver self was shorter, and flat in places where Susan had begun to curve.

"I left the rest of me at home," she said.

"You did? We went up there and rang the bell. The light went on. I think someone peeked out the peephole, then went away again."

"Susan?" Edmund said. His tone was full of wonder. He pushed his cape back and held out his hand.

She touched his palm. He closed his fingers over hers before she could pull her hand away. He drew her hand toward his face and studied it. "It's exquisite," he said. "How is it done?"

"I don't know." She restrained an impulse to say she was having an out-of-body experience. He would believe her, and then what?

"Please," he said. "It's important."

"Ask Nathan."

"Nathan?" He released Susan's hand.

"I don't think you should try this until you've had more practice," Nathan told Edmund.

Julio reached for Susan's hand. She looked at his dark face and shadowed eyes and thought about a morning a long time ago, when Juanita had plaited her hair into tight braids and loaned her one of Julio's wash-worn T-shirts and a pair of overalls. Susan and Julio had crept through bushes, finding tunnels in the blackberry brambles, carrying out a secret mission. After a very successful campaign of spying, evading the enemy, and bearing messages, they had gone home, where Juanita had scrubbed Susan clean and popped her into a pink dress just before Father got home. He had never sus-pected a thing, but he didn't like Julio being at the house, and asked Juanita to send him somewhere else. After that, Juanita only brought Julio to visit on days when she knew Father's work would keep him away from home until after it was time for Juanita to leave. They also had a plan in case of emergencies; if Father came home unexpectedly, Julio hid in the garden shed out back. It had only happened once.

They never talked about the conspiracy that defied Father behind his back. Mother never spoke of it either, though she knew Julio was still visiting the house. "You need each other," she had told Susan once.

Julio touched Susan's hand, and suddenly she felt the firm warmth of his fingers. She looked at her hand. It had reverted to flesh. "What?" he asked. He stared into her face.

"It's a little like astral projection," Nathan said.

"She's so good at it," said Edmund doubtfully.

Nathan said, "I have a lot of control over it. I won't let anything happen to her. It's just for tonight."

Edmund looked down at him. "I wish . . . " He spread his cape.

"Maybe next year." Nathan grinned.

"But—" Julio said.

"How did she get silver?" asked Deirdre, who had crowded close to Edmund while Nathan talked.

"Some things are inexplicable," Nathan said. "We have to go. Ready, Susan?"

She squeezed Julio's hand and slipped away from him to stand beside Nathan.

"Good night," Nathan said to the others. He drew Susan up into the air.

"Hey!" yelled Deirdre. "How— Hey! Come back here! Hey!"

"What? Susan!" Edmund gasped, his voice fading.

"Susan, wait," Julio cried.

They waved and flew away.

# chapter sixteen

THEY WALKED THE surface of the Columbia River. Rain changed the water's ruffled wind waves to a hissing, trembling path. Then the wind drove the clouds inland. Moonlight silvered the water and her body, and Susan felt she could melt into the river with ease; its surface met hers without pause.

They stood under the thundering torrent of Multnomah Falls, letting force and wind and water wash through them, and sound, another substance. Ferns and moss dripped and nodded on the lip of the cliff above, waving in the waterfall wind.

They climbed through apple-wine air and flew over the desert, startling a loping coyote into changing directions.

They rode a quiet wind above a winding road atop the cliffs on the north side of the river, until at last they approached a place of stones, firelight, and people.

Susan looked down on a circle of rectangular slabs as tall as two men standing one on the other's shoulders, capped by more flat slabs: a tall circle of open doorways, with firelight shining through, casting long fingers of flickering shadows on the smoothed ground.

"What is it?" she whispered. People sang in a circle within the frame of stone doorways. All around the stone circle, a darker people watched and listened. Moonlight and firelight passed through them; they cast no shadows.

"The stones, or the people?" Nathan drew her down toward Earth, outside the circle.

"The stones."

"This is a replica of Stonehenge in England. A man built it to commemorate the dead in the Great War."

"The people," she whispered. Several of the shadowless ones came toward them.

"Tonight is the crack between the old year and the new. Witches celebrate this night. Something dies, something is born, and the dead can walk. There's an energy here that attracts us. I've come to this circle the past three years."

"Nathaniel! Who's your friend?" asked a voice.

The man who had approached them was tall and hollow. He wore a tattered, old-fashioned army uniform, and had a white bandage wrapped around his head. Susan took Nathan's hand, edged closer to him.

"Don't be shy, little one. Lord knows we're past all hurting now," said the man. He touched her head. She could see through him, but his hand felt solid, though neither warm nor cold. She fought the urge to flinch away.

"Eli, this is Susan, and she's not past. Susan, Eli."

"How'd you arrange that?" Eli stooped to peer at Susan. "She looks like one of us. No shadow."

"Something I learned in the wanderings," said Nathan. "I've been saving it since the thirties. We only stopped for a minute."

"It's been a real nice ceremony so far." Eli glanced toward the firelit circle of stones, the dancing silhouettes of living humans, the more transparent forms of ghosts. A growing rhythmic voice came from the witches in the central circle, a synchronized melody of words. "Got to get back," said Eli. "It's almost as good as a bonfire. Nice to meet you, little gal." He patted Susan's head again and wandered toward the circle.

A few of the other shadowless people came to greet them, and Susan grew calm. She stooped to touch hands with a little girl, and looked at her own hand, startled to see that it had lost its steel skin and looked normal. After greetings, the others returned to the living circle, holding out their hands as if basking in warmth.

Nathan led her nearer, and she felt a force, too, and almost saw it, as she had when Edmund cast the circle: a rising spiral of energy, wide as the circle of living people at its base, narrowing in the air above them.

"Try something?" Nathan whispered to her.

She nodded.

"Do as I do," he said. He held their linked hands out, and also his other hand. She copied his movement, stared at her outstretched hands, which were somewhere between silver and flesh, a porcelain self; thinner armor, but not all the way open. She glanced down and saw that everything from her shoulders to her knees was still silver. Her arms and lower legs were almost flesh-colored.

They stood with their hands outstretched toward the spiral. Something shifted inside of her, and a stream of green light flowed from their fingertips, stained the gray-blue spiral, then blended.

They stood that way, outer additions to the circle, for a little while. Then someone in the circle directed the energy up and out. Some rose in the air, and some spread out around the circle, a pale translucent wave shot with sparks.

Some of the shadowless ghosts in the outer circle winked out when the wave flowed over them, and some grew sharper in outline. Susan swayed as the wave passed through her. It stirred her up and made her itch. Nathan's grip on her hand tightened. His eyes glowed burning blue.

The dancers collapsed, breathing deeply, and placed their hands flat on the ground. Susan let her hands drop to her sides, her left still meshed with Nathan's right. Nathan relaxed beside her.

"What was it? What did we do?" she whispered to him.

"We joined in a witch working, a blessing for the coming year and a letting go of the past."

It was so like Edmund's ritual. These were real witches, and they had done something similar to what Edmund had done. She wanted to ask him if he had learned his ritual from a live witch. If not, where? She could tell him about this—

She glanced around, saw that some of the ghosts drifted off. Were there gaps between them where others had been? "Are some of them gone?"

"One of the gifts of this time and place is the strength to move on," Nathan murmured. "We who are past but still present are tied to this Earth by something. Sometimes it's a stronger bond than we can break alone. Violence, hate, longing, love. Even if we want to leave, we can't. But this time of year, when we can wander, the ties are looser. With this kind of help, some can break free."

"Is that what you want?"

He peeked at her sideways, half a smile lifting the corner of his mouth. "Oh, no. Not now." He swung their hands. "Another gift of the working is the strength to stay and gain power and knowledge. That's the gift I choose this year."

He stared toward the people in the inner circle, some of whom stirred. He kissed his fingertips and pointed them toward the circle, then pulled Susan up into the sky again. They flew more slowly over the river down to the sea.

From the mouth of the river they turned south, drifting above coastal towns laid out like small galaxies. Headlights and taillights traveled up and down the highways, stringing towns together with a moving lace of light. Mist stole inland from the sea, hazing the moonlit landscape into fantasy. Susan heard the hush of waves breaking, muffled by the mist. She was conscious of the warmth of Nathan's hand in hers, and the salt freshness of the night air as they ghosted through it like dolphins through water. A sense of contentment welled up in her, a feeling they were headed home.

Nathan led her down through the mist into gradual darkness, homing in on House on Lee Street. They sank through the shingles together; Susan sensed the force that locked the atoms of cedar to one another. The air smelled of pencil shavings. This house had old strength built into it, and old and new magic, and an accumulation of life force that spoke to her, saying no matter what else happened to her, she would always be welcome here. House's heart had a chamber that would hold her, wrap her round with a steady pulse, and each beat would be love, and the heart would never die.

They went to Nathan's room, which had become Susan's, and sat on the bed beside each other, surrounded by the breath and pulse of House. It made a living warmth that drove off the sea chill. Susan relaxed.

Susan's hand rested in Nathan's. She wanted to lean on him. But she couldn't lean on anyone, could she?

She sighed. In the pale green light that she was not sure she saw with her eyes, she could see herself, and she saw that the steel skin had vanished from her arms and legs and the place over her heart. She touched her face. Her fingertips sensed the soft peach-skin of her cheeks, and her face perceived the warm pads of her fingertips. She touched Nathan's lips, felt them form a smile.

She flexed her fingers, marveled that his hand felt warm. "I bet most people don't have first dates like this."

He laughed. Then his face stilled, and he stared at her intently. "We can't—" he said.

She closed her eyes. "I thought we could do anything," she whispered, and then fear at her own words flowed through her, freezing syrup that turned her to stone. Anything included too much.

"No," he said. "We only have tonight, and tomorrow we have to deal with the consequences of whatever we do now. I promised I wouldn't hurt you, if I can figure out what hurts. I need to honor that promise. Some things hurt a lot more after they're over. What we can do that won't hurt is sit side by side." His fingers moved in hers. "Touch, this much. That's enough for now."

# chapter seventeen

SHADOW SUSAN HAD put herself to bed.

Just before dawn, Nathan and Susan stood on the dusty-rose carpet and looked at the body's sleeping face. She really was beautiful, Susan thought, detached. Poor fairy princess.

Nathan walked to the bed. "She's awfully lively, for a shadow." He frowned, then turned to Susan. "You'd better hop back in while I still have the power to put you together."

"What would happen if I didn't? Couldn't she go through the rest of her days alone? Couldn't I—couldn't I stay with you?"

"You can't do it that way. I'm not sure what would happen if you and your shadow stay apart, but I think it involves dissolving, for both of you."

"I'd like to dissolve." Susan laid her hand on the shadow's face. Her hand passed through it as Nathan's hand had passed through Trudie's face. She jerked her hand back.

"Please," Nathan said. "Please don't dissolve. I'd miss you."

Susan smiled at him, then looked away.

Was that a strong enough reason?

Then she thought: He had power over her. He could force her back into herself, even if she didn't want to go. If he did that to her, she would lose everything, trust and friendship and refuge and the whole of the night. If he forced her to do anything, he would be too much like Father.

How could he not force her, if she left the choice up to him? He had promised not to hurt her, and dissolving would probably hurt more than losing trust. It would be more permanent. Maybe.

She climbed onto the bed and back inside her shadow. It was like passing through a light drizzle of sand. Nathan touched her head and back, whispered words. She flexed her hand, pulled it out from under the covers, looked at it.

She rubbed her eyes. Nathan was still there, standing on the rose-colored rug. She sat up, discovered that Shadow Susan had dressed in one of her fleecier nightgowns. She held out her hand to Nathan. He laid his palm on hers, but she felt the warmth leach from his hand.

"I have to go," he murmured. Even his touch faded. She forgot: She was not holding the bone.

"It was the best night of my life," she said.

He smiled. Dawn struck through the pink curtains. He faded from solid to shadow to nothing. She pressed her fingers against the inside corners of her eyes to keep tears from leaking out.

"Did you finish your Constitution paper? You certainly worked late enough," her father said.

Susan handed him the paper she had found on her desk and sat down to her bowl of cereal. Mother smiled at her and passed her the milk pitcher. "Thank you," Susan said, and ate while Father read.

"This is very good," he said, "very good. I don't know why you wrote it in pencil, though. If you have time in homeroom today, you should copy it over in pen before you turn it in. Is the deadline today? Maybe you should type it tonight, if it can wait another day. What have you got in your hand, Princess?"

"What?" Susan looked at her spoon, poised above her bowl of Cheerios, then held it up.

"The other hand."

She felt a familiar knotting in her midsection. Why hadn't she left the bone in her school bag? Father watched everything she did, especially on his I-see-all mornings. "It's part of a project for science class," she said. "We're learning the bones of the human body. I took this one home by mistake, I guess on Friday." She opened her hand. She felt queasy. If he touched it—she imagined some sort of contamination, as if his personality were a form of radiation that could poison Nathan.

"Which bone is it?" he asked, plucking it from her hand.

She swallowed. "The metacarpal." She had looked it up in the school library. "It's a bone in the thumb."

"I think I should have a talk with the headmaster." Her father frowned at the bone. "I'm not sure I like the thought of hands-on teaching in anatomy."

"We're not really supposed to touch them." Susan tasted her breakfast trying to come back up. "That one just came loose, and I was going to tidy it up, but the bell rang. I guess I just put it in my pocket."

"What pocket?" said Father.

"The one in my plaid skirt."

"Weren't you wearing navy on Friday?"

"Oh. Maybe that's right. I found the bone in one of my skirt pockets today when I was turning them inside out. It's wash day."

He gave her back the bone. "Well, make sure you return it today. It's a filthy thing to have around the house."

"Where on Earth did you get that costume? It was so cool! You should wear it to school so everybody else can see it!" Pam said that afternoon in the locker room.

"It was tissue-paper thin," Susan told Pam. "I don't think I could put it on again."

"It was gorgeous. You guys, you should have seen Susan's costume," Pam said to the locker room at large. "It was like something out of a comic book. All silver."

"What neighborhood did you do?" someone asked.

"Pam's house was the only one I went to," Susan
said, gazing at the floor. "We mostly did other things."

"Was he ever cute," said Pam.

" 'He?' " Their voices were openly incredulous.

Susan smiled slowly, feeling a strange new blossom-
ing of satisfaction. They teased her for his name and
address, as they often teased one another. She could not
stop smiling.

Edmund, Deirdre, and Julio came out of the trees by
the school driveway.

"Are you all right?"

"Where'd you go?"

"What did it feel like?"

Susan hugged her school bag to her chest. The smile
had not left her face since gym. Nathan's bone was
secure inside her hand. She began to walk, and they fell
into step.

"Susan," said Julio, touching her shoulder. "Susan?"

"How did you turn silver?" Edmund asked.

"I don't know, I don't know." She alternated walking
steps with skipping steps.

"At least you're still alive," Julio muttered so low
she almost didn't hear him.

Her gaze sharpened, but he turned his head away.

He'd been worried about her. Well, he didn't have to
worry anymore. She was back to normal. Back inside
her shadow self. She still had memories, though. She
skipped again.

They reached the end of the school driveway. Susan glanced toward town and the video arcade. She hadn't collected data on Friday, too afraid to stretch her freedom so far it would snap, and she would lose it. She should go today. She needed to chart data on a regular basis or her science project would have holes in it. Father would complain and suspect the worst.

Not that he knew what she was working on, exactly. She had told him she was studying the effects of computers on people, and she had shown him all the things she was charting over time, how she had selected five subjects to observe, and what behavior factors she was watching. He checked her charts every day she was late coming home.

He would have to know, when she put together her paper and display, exactly what she had been studying. But by that time, she would have had a whole month to . . .

To build memories that would sustain her, like her memory of that one magical day at the beach with Aunt Caroline.

To get the rest of her month, she needed to keep collecting new data. She should go to the arcade today.

But she couldn't wait to see Nathan again. She had felt so close to him last night. Now she was back inside herself. Would that change things? She hoped it wouldn't. She needed to know, either way. She walked with the other three away from town and toward the haunted house.

"Where did you go?" asked Deirdre.

"We flew through clouds. We walked on the river. We stood under a waterfall. It was lovely."

"You're not going to float up into the air again, are you?" Julio asked.

Susan paused as they reached Lee Street. She glanced at him, her smile dimming. "No."

Julio raised his hands before him, then clenched them into fists. "It's not that I want you to . . . It's just . . . Oh, Susan."

"Spit it out," said Deirdre. "You're making me nervous."

Julio looked at her, let his hands fall to his sides. "Never mind."

They passed through the sagging gate and turned onto the bramble path to House. They had taken three steps before Susan noticed the tingling in her hand. "Wait."

They paused. Susan looked over her shoulder toward the road.

"Oh, jeez," said Deirdre. "We're getting careless."

They waited a moment. Then Trudie stepped out from behind a tree. "All right. I wanted to catch you red-handed." Her green eyes blazed. "Red-footed. Whatever. You *are* coming here."

"What's it to you?" asked Deirdre.

"I suppose you think you own the place."

"Of course we don't own it," Deirdre said. "We're invited guests. You heard Miss Manners here the first time you came." She gestured toward Susan. "A proper introduction and an engraved invitation get you in.

Otherwise, forget it. He's not very nice to uninvited guests."

"He?" said Trudie. Her freckles blazed against suddenly pale skin.

"The owner," Deirdre said. "The other guy who met you at the door. What did he do to you, anyway? Susan never told us."

"He hypnotized me. I'd like to see him try it again. I'd just like to." Her voice came out strong, but her face stayed pale.

Deirdre looked at Susan, who glanced at her hand. The bone had stopped tingling.

Julio said, "Trudie, why are you doing this?"

"Doing what?" She stuck her chin out.

"Following us. Pestering us. Trying to hurt us."

"You fascinate me."

"How can we stop doing that?" asked Edmund.

Trudie shook her head, smiling. "Not going to happen. I want to know everything about you. It's not just you, of course; I study everyone I know. But right now you guys are the most interesting subjects I have."

"Subjects? What makes you think you're the queen of us?" Deirdre asked.

"Not that kind of subject. I'm talking about science experiments. I study how people respond to stress. It's my life's work."

"If there's no stress, you make some up?" Julio asked.

Trudie smiled some more. "That's a variable I have some control over."

"Lying to us? Making us think we hated each other? That's your idea of fun?" Edmund asked.

Trudie's smile didn't waver. "It's interesting to find out how fragile people are, how to turn friends into enemies. How easy is it for a relationship to break up? You guys fascinate me because you didn't fall apart. Yet. I want to know your secret."

"So you want to experiment on us," Deirdre said. "Too damn bad. We're not interested in helping you with your 'science project,' okay? Leave!"

"Why should I make it easy on you? Just standing here I'm applying stress. What will you do in response?"

"How about *we* leave?" said Edmund. "Let's go inside. House won't let her in."

"House," said Trudie. "Is that a name? The house's name is House? How geeky is that?"

Edmund turned away from her and headed through the brambles around the side of the house. Julio and Deirdre followed him.

Susan stayed.

"Yes," Trudie said, "I was wondering how you fit in. Where did you come from? How could you possibly join their tight little group? They're so happy with each other they don't let anybody else in."

"Why do people stay together?" Susan asked. "Is that something you've studied?"

Trudie's eyebrows flickered, up, down. "Not specifically. My theory is nobody ever stays together. I've tested it a lot, and it's usually true."

"My parents." Susan's voice choked itself.

Trudie took a step closer, her green eyes bright. "Yes?"

Susan swallowed, shook her head.

Trudie's eyes narrowed. "Invite me over to your house and I'll observe them and get back to you."

Susan swiped a hand across her eye, shook her head again. "Never mind," she whispered.

Something tight in Trudie's posture loosened a little. One shoulder lowered. "Yeah," she said. "Okay. My theory is that parents are weird anyway. At least you have two, right? My dad left when I was six."

"Did you figure out why?"

"Oh, sure. Basically it was me." Trudie smiled. "That's what I do. Make people leave."

"That's your nightmare," Susan whispered. "I see."

"What are you talking about? That's my power."

"Turn your nightmare into your power." Susan stared at the ground, her hand tight around Nathan's bone. Her nightmare: Father finding out what she'd been doing for the last week. Father deciding Mother needed to be punished. Father meting out the punishment. What Susan had done wrong this past week was so vast compared to anything she'd done before that this—

Mother.

*My nightmare is to cause pain to the one I love most. My power—*

*My power—*

*My power is pain. What can I do with my power?*

"But you—no, that's not what I— Hmm," said Trudie. "Do you have an analytic mind, too?"

Susan grasped a bramble and pressed a thorn into her palm, then opened her hand and watched the blood bead. No feeling accompanied the wounding. Mute, she held her hand out toward Trudie.

"What did you do to yourself?" Trudie asked.

Twice when Susan had spoken to Trudie before, she had pretended to be Mother. If she was herself, she would just shut up and not talk at all. But she wanted —

She wanted to talk.

Why did she want to talk to this person, the one her friends told her was mean and untrustworthy?

Matching darkness. House sense almost worked on Trudie: Susan could sense empty places inside Trudie like the dark rooms inside herself.

"It doesn't hurt," she heard herself saying in a voice she almost didn't recognize: her own. "Yet it must hurt. It's a wound, and wounds are supposed to hurt. This blood is a signal, but if I don't look at it, and I can't feel it, I won't know there's anything wrong. What if it got infected? What if my heart stopped and I never noticed?"

"What are you saying?" Trudie whispered.

"I don't have words like you. I don't know what this means or how to say it, but there's something—something." Her own voice. "We walk around with these wounds in our side, but we're not allowed to talk about them. It's not polite. It's wrong. But they're there. We have to do something about them. The—the infection has to get out somehow, or if it's locked inside, the pressure gets too strong, and something breaks—" She swayed a little. She dropped her school bag and put both hands over her face, the left hand fisted around the bone, the right hand open—

—and Nathan was beside her. His arms went around her and he supported her. Trudie stepped forward, too, reached out.

Susan felt the sobs inside her, pressing against the roof of her mouth, knocking against the inside of her skull. Her throat closed on them.

"It's locked inside? She has something locked inside?" Trudie asked.

"Yes," said Nathan. Susan sensed them looking at each other, but she was too busy holding on to all the pieces of herself to try to understand. She felt close to crumbling. Nathan stroked her head; his caress was chill and gentle, like the embrace of a quiet current in a stream. He drew her arm around his shoulder, wrapped his arm around her waist. "Come inside," he said to Trudie.

Trudie picked up Susan's school bag and followed him up the porch stairs to the front door.

# chapter eighteen

"I'M ALL RIGHT," said Susan. She scrubbed at her hand with a crumpled tissue.

Trudie, sitting on the living room floor beside her, handed her another tissue from the school bag. "There's a little blood on your cheek."

Susan spat on the tissue, then rubbed her cheek, looked to Trudie for a nod that would tell her she had gotten the spot off. "Let me." Trudie took the tissue back. Susan sat quiet, eyes closed, as the other girl touched her face with the damp tissue. It was only the Shadow this stranger touched, Susan's outside edges—Father's property. She was a provisional tenant. She smiled and opened her eyes.

"I'm sorry," she said. "I think I got a little carried away."

"Kind of divine madness," said Trudie. "I wish you hadn't stopped. I think you were saying something, but you didn't finish it."

"Are you speaking as a scientist?" Susan flexed her hands, then closed the left around the bone in her lap.

Her armor formed again, the silver layer under her skin. Nathan stood beside her.

"No." Trudie turned away. She shifted her shoulders, then shook her head and turned back. "We haven't been properly introduced," she said, looking from Susan to Nathan.

Startled, Susan recognized her own tones in Trudie's voice: Trudie imitated Susan imitating Mother.

"We don't have a hostess to do that, so let's be improper." Nathan sat beside Susan on the floor. "My name is Nathan Blacksmith."

"Trudie Adams." She stuck out her hand.

"That doesn't work," Nathan said. "Remember?"

"Oh, God." Trudie jerked her hand back. She looked at the ceiling, then at the corners. Her face tightened. "You mean that wasn't just hypnosis?"

"It wasn't."

"Oh, God. I don't know if I can deal with this. Way too far from rationality." She reached out, tried to touch his knee. Her hand passed through him. She held her hand out and stared at it, then looked at him. "Mirrors?" she said, with no real hope in her voice.

"No."

"I don't think I believe in you." She rubbed one hand with the other, as if to make sure both were real and solid.

"That's all right. This is Susan," said Nathan, laying a hand on Susan's head.

"You can touch her."

"I can touch her while she's holding one of my bones."

Trudie blinked. "That white thing?"

Susan opened her hand. The bone lay quiet on her palm.

"May I try?" Trudie held out her hand. Susan dropped the bone into it. Holding the bone in her left hand, Trudie extended her right again, and this time Nathan shook it. "Hmm," said Trudie. "You feel too cold, but you *are* there. I can't think of a scientific explanation for that." She covered her eyes with her hand and took a deep breath. "Okay. I'm not going to think about it." She took another deep breath, lowered her hand, and glanced around the room. "What happened to all the furniture?"

"It was just shadows of what used to be here. Susan did it."

Trudie tugged on her own hair. "Could you do it again?" she asked, sitting still.

"Oh, why not?" Susan retrieved the bone from Trudie and opened her house sense wide.

Shock jolted through her. The presence of House was much stronger all around her; she realized that Halloween night had not been a dream. House breathed for her. It welcomed her in its heart. Its pulse throbbed in the floor; its strength and affection surrounded her. She looked at Nathan, wide-eyed. Half his mouth quirked up in a smile.

"Susan?" said Trudie.

Susan remembered: She had been about to conjure up furniture. She closed her eyes and, with her house sense, reached into the repository of energy and images in the walls, summoned forth the living room furniture. When everything felt correct in the space around her, she opened her eyes, to see Trudie touching the red-and-blue carpet.

"It feels real," Trudie said, wonder in her tone. "But I saw it appear. I feel like I'm in the *Arabian Nights* or something. This is so unscientific. Maybe I'm dreaming." She scrambled to her feet and walked over to the piano. She lifted the cover over the keys and pressed down middle C. The note sang in the room, sweet and ancient. "I can touch these things," she said. She pulled out the bench and sat down, then played "Chopsticks." "It's solid. I could take it home." She reached up and ran her hand through the beaded fringe of the lamp that sat on the piano. "Is it like fairy gold? Does it turn to leaves and mud the next morning? I can't believe I'm even asking these questions."

"Where did this stuff come from? Susan— Oh, Trudie! You're still here?" Julio said from the door.

"I got the invitation and the introduction. Check out the piano," said Trudie. "Try it, Julio."

"How could you invite her in?" Deirdre asked Nathan.

"We needed her," he said. Julio went to the piano and stood beside it until Trudie relinquished the piano bench to him.

Edmund went to the mantel, looked up at the portrait, then focused on the clock below it. Above a round white clock face with Roman numerals on it, a bronze horse in midgallop supported a bronze rider who held a lariat in his upraised hand. "What a weird thing," said Edmund.

"Mother bought it during the Roosevelt years," Nathan said. "The strenuous life. I loved that clock."

Julio glanced at the rest of them, played a scale up and down the keyboard of the piano, then launched into a Chopin waltz. Trudie stood behind him, watching his hands on the keys.

Deirdre, still glowering, walked over to where Nathan sat on the rug beside Susan. "How could you need her?" she asked under the music.

"The rest of you had gone inside, and Susan needed help."

For a moment, Deirdre glared at Susan, then her expression softened. "Are you all right now?" She dropped to sit cross-legged on the rug.

"I'm fine. I don't think she's as bad as you think. She was telling me something, Dee. And I was trying to say something." Susan clenched both her hands into fists and set them on her knees.

"Something about your nightmare?"

Susan felt her breath moving in and out. "Yes," she said, after a few deep breaths. "She has one, too."

Deirdre stared into her eyes. "Well, I'm glad if she does. I hope she's got some kind of big, awful problem. I hate all that 'superior intellect' stuff. I think it's stupid. My dad says some people are too smart for their own good. I mean, what good does it do her to make us jerk around like puppets? The best trick would be if she could make us want to like her again; I don't think she's smart enough for that."

"Does she make you feel stupid?" Susan asked. Darkness hovered over her like a storm waiting to break. It had come close several times today, but every time she stopped thinking about herself and concentrated on someone else, it went away again. Susan leaned toward Deirdre and tried to think herself into the other girl's shoes.

"When she talks about us as subjects in some dumb experiment? What do you think?"

"I think that's just— It's just words." Then she touched her lip. "Word Magic." Dangerous stuff.

"But she really did do what she said. She came to school. She looked around at how people related to each other. Then she did these calculated things. She broke up three couples. Not the usual way—not by stealing the guy. She'd just tell one of them what she heard the other one say. Sometimes it was even true. All these people who had been having a great time, suddenly they hated each other. She almost did that to us, Susan."

"Yes, but she didn't succeed."

"Because we talk to each other," said Deirdre. She glanced at Nathan, then back at Susan. "She uses Word Magic, but we do, too. Sometimes I think all the problems in the world come from people not talking to each other. If you could talk about your nightmare . . . "

Susan looked at her clenched fists. She thought about living in her father's house, and she felt her throat close, her breath shorten. The storm was above her, all around her, not as friendly as the rain clouds she had mingled with on Halloween. And the storm broke.

"See what happens when Princess cries?" Father's voice asked. She reached to touch the purple place on Mother's arm. She knew Father had said other things to her, things she couldn't even think about before. This time, she let them drift back to her.

"Everything that happens here is your fault, Princess. The evil is in you. It reaches out through me to hurt your mother. You force me to act. When you're perfectly good, it will stop, and we'll all be happy."

Perfectly good. Or dead.

She looked at the room, her friends. The music Julio made swept around her. Deirdre watched her with compassionate eyes, waiting for Word Magic to free Susan from a nightmare.

She thought about her first deception—telling Father she was going to the library, and then coming here. She thought about the next deceptions, more by omission than by outright lie: she let her father think she was spending her afternoons doing research for her project, and only a little piece of that was true. She had not told him the exact nature of her research, knowing he probably wouldn't approve. She had never told him about her visits to the haunted house. What if he found out? What if he found out she had friends now? What if she told them anything and he found out?

"If you tell anyone what happens in our home, it will kill your mother," her father's voice whispered. He had said that while he was hugging her good-bye on her first day of first grade. He had told her again one morning at breakfast, after such an awful night—what had Susan done that Father had to correct her through Mother? She couldn't even remember—that Mother was too ill to come down for breakfast. "Princess, you love your mother, don't you?"

Her stomach cramped. She clamped her arms over her stomach and curled up around the central knot of pain. Pain, a pain she could feel. She sank deep under the surface of a wonderful fiery sea of pain that consumed everything else.

At last, at last, she could feel the pain herself, didn't have to watch it happening to Mother. Maybe if she felt enough pain, Father would never have to hurt Mother again. She clutched herself, pulled pain close, dived into it. Score my skin. Beat my muscles and bruise my bones. Let me take this, let it never happen to Mother again. Punish *me*. *I'm* the one who did everything wrong—

She floated in the sea of fire, welcomed the waves. Come into me. Come over me. Swallow me. Hurt *me*.

Hurt *him*.

No, she couldn't ever have *that* thought—

All this lovely fire, if only she could turn it toward—
Unthinkable.

Her breathing was ragged, choked. She lost the calm
fire that burned her from the inside out. The fine power
of perfect pain ebbed.

There were voices, saying things she didn't try to
understand, and touches she barely felt. Finally a sense
of warmth and love seeped in around the edges of the
pain, diluting it until it was too weak to clench her into
a fetal fist. She relaxed, and discovered she could
breathe.

When she opened her eyes, she looked up into a lot
of faces. She felt embarrassed that so many people had
seen her lose control.

"Are you okay?" Trudie asked, smoothing the hair
away from Susan's forehead.

"What?" Susan blinked, then yawned, covering her
mouth with her left hand, still tightly clenched around
Nathan's bone. "I'm sorry. I don't know what happened." She looked at her watch, noticed that her arm
was dirty. "Oh, look at the time. I've got to get home and
change."

"Is she crazy?" Deirdre asked Nathan in despair.

"No. Well, in a way. But she does have to get home."

Susan sat up, looked around the room. The furniture had vanished. The floor was carpeted only by dust.
"Oh, dear. I'm sorry."

"Susan?" Edmund gripped her right hand. "What
happened, really? What do you remember?"

She shook her head. "Nothing."

"You just had a fit," Deirdre said. "We should get you to a doctor."

"Oh, my stomach hurt. It hurts sometimes. Isn't that odd? Nothing else does. I'm sorry I lost track of the furniture." She looked around at them. Too many people staring at her. Too many people who wanted to know all the things she couldn't speak of. She had to get out of here. "Julio, would you please walk me home?"

"Yes." He took her hand and helped her up.

"Julio, you know, don't you? You know what the nightmare is," said Deirdre. "Tell us. Can't you see she needs help? We should call somebody."

"I don't know for sure what it is," he said. Trudie handed him Susan's school bag. He slid the strap over his shoulder, then brushed some of the dust off Susan's back. "I only suspect. Susan has to decide what to do. You know you have a safe place here, Susan."

"I love this house." Susan felt House's presence all around her. She knew House had driven out her pain. She smiled at Nathan.

"You can't just walk away from us like that," Deirdre cried. "We want to help! Tell us what to do."

"I can't. I really can't. I have to go."

Edmund touched Deirdre's shoulder. "Let it go for now. Come upstairs with me, Dee."

# chapter nineteen

FATHER HAD COME home early.

As she climbed the hill beside Julio, Susan glanced up at the house and saw Father standing at one of the narrow living room windows, looking down.

Susan touched Julio's arm. "You'd better go home."

He looked up, saw her father. "Oh, no. You aren't safe. Let me come with you."

"It would just make things worse." She looked at her sleeves. Dust darkened them. She touched her head, felt snarls in her hair. "Go home, please, Julio."

"Don't let anything happen to you. Remember you're not alone anymore. Do you want me to wait near the house? I can hide out in the garden shed if you want."

She stared into his eyes.

All her silver armor was in place. Nathan's bone was hidden in a pocket in her school bag. She felt a new distance from Julio. If she leaned on him, it would only bring him trouble, and she didn't want to have to worry about anyone else getting hurt.

She knew now that her own territory, her inner self, could come loose in a discrete package. She could leave her body behind, the way she had on Halloween. She had a place to go.

But what would happen to Mother?

She clutched her head. "There's a decision I have to make."

Father's gaze was on them. He would be wondering what they were saying. Perhaps in his years of observing her he had learned to read her lips.

"A decision," Julio repeated.

She wondered what would have happened if she had come straight home today. Her house sense would have warned her when Father came home, and she would have had time to straighten her clothes and sit at her desk before he came upstairs. Everything could have stayed the way it was.

The way it was. "I'm so tired."

"Yes," Julio said.

"I don't want to live like this anymore."

Father's head bent toward them. He stood so still. Susan felt as if his paralysis had infected her.

"I know it's tough for you at home, but now you can get away. Doesn't that help?"

"Now I can get away," she whispered.

Julio gripped her arm. "That's not what I mean."

Staring up at her house with its long, narrow windows, Susan said, "Now he knows I've been gone. He won't let me get away anymore. He'll lock all the doors." He would be angry. He was already angry, she could see it in his squared shoulders. He was angry, and Mother would suffer, and—acid poured into Susan's stomach again. She pressed her hands against her belly.

"No more free afternoons," she whispered around the tightness in her throat. "No more haunted house. No more Nathan."

"He can't do that, can he?"

"Of course he can. He can stop my body from going anywhere."

"Of course he can," Julio echoed, "somehow. I don't know how. I just know it hurts you."

"It doesn't hurt *me*."

"Of course it does. Susan—I know you had a good time last night, going out with Nathan. You were like a ghost yourself, right? But that's not the answer."

"Why not?" she whispered.

"It's not. It can't be. You're my friend. I don't want you to die."

"Living is too hard."

"It's hard right now, but if you can hold out until you're eighteen, you can get away from here. We'll help you live through it."

"He won't let you help me. He'll never let me leave as long as I'm alive. And anyway, I'm not the one who needs help." If only she knew how to help Mother.

Julio stared past her, up at her father in the window. "But—"

"Go home, Julio. I'll tell him I was working late on my science project." She didn't have the notes to substantiate the lie today. She hadn't collected data or written it down, even fake data. Her father might believe her even so, if only Julio hadn't come home with her. Father thought she had stopped seeing him years ago.

"Don't go home, Susan. Come with me. You can stay with me and Mama. I know that cop, Jeff, the guy who came to the house. You tell him what happens at your house, and he'll take care of you."

"No. Mother—"

"Come on. You can't go back." He took her arm and led her away, down the hill.

She glanced over her shoulder at the living room windows. Father was gone. She let Julio lead her down the hill; another delay, another case of letting someone else take responsibility.

What about Mother?

She felt tired.

Father's gray sedan coasted down the driveway and came to a silent halt in the street beside them. The passenger's-side window went down with a quiet electric purr. "Where are you going?" Father asked in his deceptively calm prosecuting attorney's voice.

Susan was too weary to think up an answer.

"I'm taking her to my place, sir," said Julio.

"Get your hands off my daughter. Go home and tell your mother she's fired. Princess, get into the car."

"She's coming home with me, sir," said Julio.

"Princess, you know what this means to your mother. Get in the car."

Susan tested her armor again. Solid. No feeling got through; no anger, fear, nor pain. She twisted her arm free of Julio's grasp and climbed into the car.

"I'm calling the police," yelled Julio, as Father made the window on Susan's side of the car go up. Father gunned the motor and swerved toward Julio, who jumped over the bank and disappeared.

Father did not stop to see what had become of him. He did a smooth three-point turnaround, and the car glided up the driveway and into the garage. A press of a button, and the garage door closed behind them.

"Where have you been, Princess?" Father asked in the darkness. "What have you and that boy been doing? How long has this been going on?"

His voice came to her across a distance. Susan leaned back in her seat, noticing that she could not feel the thick plush. Nothing penetrated her awareness but the sound of his voice.

"How did you get so filthy?" he asked.

"Where's Mother?"

"She's at the hospital."

For a panicked moment, she thought Father had already done something drastic to Mother. Then she remembered it was Monday. Mother did volunteer work at the hospital Monday afternoons.

"Come into the house," he said.

Her body followed him into the house. He paused in

the front hall, as if uncertain of his next move. Then he led her into his study and closed the curtains.

She stood in the center of his fleecy beige rug, facing his desk, an enormous asymmetrical modern piece of blond wood with all the corners rounded off. He sat in his desk chair.

"Susan, I love you more than anything else in my life," he said. "You are my hope for the future. Ever since you were born I've done my utmost to protect you from evil influences and turn you into the best person you could possibly be. Most of the time, you are beautiful, well mannered, intelligent, well groomed, and responsible. You are growing into a fine young lady. You don't want to upset that process, do you? You don't want to spend time with unworthy people in dirty places. That sort of filth is communicable, Princess."

He picked up a Venetian glass paperweight, pink and white bubble-flowers trapped in a crystal globe, and stared into it. He took out his handkerchief, set the paperweight on the desk, and wiped off his own finger-prints. "Sometimes the dirt is just on the outside. You can still clean it off. There's hope."

"Let me take a shower and change my clothes," Susan said.

He looked at her. He had gone white around the mouth. "You do that," he said, "and remember, when you do something wrong, it reflects on your mother. She's already flawed. We use her as a lesson. The evil in you comes out on her body, Susan, so that you may look at it and learn. Your mother's life would be much easier if you would learn not to make these mistakes."

She turned away, then heard her own voice, high and thin. "I try so hard, Daddy."

"I know you do. For a while there, you were succeeding. Let's make that happen again. Go on upstairs now, Princess, and straighten up."

The front doorbell rang as she reached the landing.

"Good evening, officer," her father's voice said. "You've had a complaint? About my daughter? She's fine. Susan!"

She walked down the stairs again. She felt as if her knees wouldn't bend. Each step jolted her.

"Susan, the officer wants to know if you're all right, honey," said Father. "As you can see, Officer, she's been roughhousing a little, but she was just on her way upstairs to take a shower."

"Is that true, miss?" She recognized his voice, though she'd only heard it through walls and floors before. It was Jeff Hawkins. She came closer and looked at him. He had a broad-boned face that looked as if he hadn't grown into it yet, and narrow blue eyes. She wondered what Julio had told him.

"Yes, sir," she said.

"Glad to hear it, miss. Sorry to trouble you, sir. We had that report—"

"It's best to verify these things," said her father. "It would be hard to live with yourself if you discovered you had been negligent."

"Yeah." Jeff sounded surprised. He took a last look at Susan, and she looked back at him, thinking about Word Magic. Father was a master of Word Magic. Susan remembered trips to the hospital with Mother and Father in the middle of the night, how Father would talk to the doctors and explain how clumsy Mother had been. The doctors always believed him. Sometimes they kidded Mother about how accident-prone she was.

Susan was paralyzed. She had no Word Magic. She couldn't think of anything to say to Jeff that would tell him what was happening, let him know she needed help. He would go, leave her here alone with Father, leave her to fight to get her old life back again, her old unbearable life, so much worse now that she knew there were other ways to live.

He would walk away.

Jeff touched his cap. "Well, good night, sir. Miss."

"Good night, Officer." Father smiled as he shut the door. He gave Susan a friendly nod. "I really think you can be saved," he said.

When she reached the top of the stairs, she went first into her parents' bedroom, trusting her house sense when it told her Father had gone back into his study. She searched her father's sink for razor blades, but he used an electric shaver. She would have to find something else.

Later that night, after supper and homework, Susan tried to sleep, but she could hear the sound, through her mother's and her own closets, of something slapping against flesh, and her mother's small, anguished whimpers. Susan flinched at each sound. By the time the sounds ended, she had curled up into a small, trembling ball.

Mother never blamed her. Somehow that was worse than anything else.

When her house sense told her it was safe, Susan got up and dressed.

# chapter twenty

SHE LEFT A pillow-and-sweater shape like Shadow Susan under the covers in her bed, and sneaked downstairs in her stocking feet, carrying her shoes in one hand and Nathan's bone in the other. Time for it to go home.

The kitchen was beneath her room. Father was in his study at the front of the house, chamber music playing softly. He would be studying legal briefs for tomorrow's cases, the way he did every weeknight, although on the nights when he beat Mother, he went to bed a little earlier than usual. It was only around nine-thirty P.M., but Susan didn't think waiting would help. If she waited longer, he would come upstairs. It took him a while to prepare for bed, and he kept coming to her bedroom door and peering in at her between preparations. She always pretended she was asleep, but she felt his gaze on her, its savoring, possessive quality.

Would the shape of her shadow fool him into thinking she was there? She had covered Sweater Susan's head with a sheet. Sometimes she slept that way, completely buried in blankets, especially on nights when Father beat Mother.

When he discovered she wasn't in her bed—

He had already hurt Mother horribly tonight. He had never hit her two times in the same night. If he did, could Mother survive?

Susan couldn't stand these questions anymore.

She slipped into the kitchen, went to the counter, and eased open the drawer where Juanita kept the knives.

Father had fired Juanita this afternoon because Julio had tried to help Susan. Juanita wouldn't suffer because her son was unwise in his friends. Lots of people wanted to hire Juanita. She stayed on with the Backstroms because—

Well, maybe because she was watching out for Susan.

Susan stared into the cutlery drawer, struggled for breath. Juanita was one of the few people Susan loved, one of the few people who loved Susan. Susan's eyes heated.

What if Father tried to ruin Juanita?

Susan couldn't think of anything she could do to stop him. She couldn't think at all.

She took a really sharp knife, wrapped the blade in a silk handkerchief, and put it in her coat pocket.

The kitchen door opened silently to outdoors. Juanita kept it oiled, knowing that in this wet climate, everything rusted, given the opportunity. Susan slipped out of the house, eased the door shut behind her, stepped into her shoes, and sneaked down the embankment to the road.

She pulled sea air inside her in deep, long breaths, thinking of these breaths as her last. She let her armor drop, enjoyed every scent in the air, tree, grass, woodsmoke, damp asphalt, rain, sea, wet wood siding, and the spice of tanbark around the small juniperbush border of their yard. The night air felt soft against her face, with only the faintest breeze. Her wool coat warmed her, though between the hem of her dress and the tops of her knee socks she felt how cool the night was. She hugged herself, then ran on the verge down the hill, her steps nearly silent on the soft grass and dirt.

Around the curve from her father's house, she stepped out into the street, enjoying the impact of her feet on the pavement. Her hard-soled shoes made flat slapping noises. She scuffed and shuffled, destroying the polished finish on the leather uppers. Tonight was a good night to wear things out, since she wouldn't need them in the morning. She ran under a sky cast in clouds, deep folds of slate gray interrupted by rivers of pale electric blue: moonlight, filtering through the deeps and shallows of a milky river.

On Lee Street, most of the porch lights were out. One leaked light across a dew-drenched lawn. The lawn needed cutting: grass blades stood up in wet spikes of shadow. Susan paused, studied the lawn and how the light, dimmed by distance, touched her shoes. Then she walked on into darkness.

Once she stepped through the gate, her house sense opened, and she walked the bramble path without needing to watch where she was going. House opened the front door for her, but she paused on the porch to take off her shoes. There were too many knots of warm energy inside House. Sorting through her impressions, she realized there were four living people in House already.

Her euphoria evaporated, leaving weariness in its place. She had made her decision. She didn't feel like having any more arguments.

Edmund and Deirdre were in the attic. Julio sat in the pantry near the back porch. Music came from that direction; Susan recognized the sound of the mandolin Julio had found in House. Surprisingly, Trudie was curled in a corner of the housekeeper's bedroom, a dark little room under the stairs they had never explored.

House was especially alive tonight. Its web of energy pulsed so strongly she could almost see a greenish radiance in the hall. Nathan coalesced beside her, an unbreathing extension of House. "I haven't talked to any of them," he said. "What do they think will happen?"

"Father saw me come home today with Julio," Susan whispered. "I never want to go back to his house again. I want to be here with you and House. I want to be dead,

Nathan." She put a hand up to her cheek, surprised by a tear. But of course, she had been discarding her armor with every step she took away from her father's house. She didn't expect to need it again.

"Oh, Susan." She heard dismay in his voice, and wished she had kept some of the armor.

"You don't want me here?" She called on her house sense, seeking its mood. House welcomed her with warmth and an almost proprietary affection. Whatever she wanted to do, House wouldn't argue with her.

"It's not that. I don't want you letting loose of life. Listen: What I did was a mistake. The rewards of this existence are few and far between. Look how long I had to wait for you. . . ."

"I'm not looking for rewards," she said, her voice rising. "I just want the punishment to stop."

Silence resounded after she spoke. The moment of hush was as tense and timeless as the space between the end of a concert and the start of applause. House held its breath.

A lance of light laid an oblong on the hall floor. Scuffling steps approached. "Susan?" said Trudie's voice, thick with drowsiness. She splashed the light across Susan's shoes. "What are you doing here?"

"Isn't that an open secret? Everybody else is here." She felt furious. "You can come out now."

Julio came from the dining room. "I didn't think you'd use the front door." He held another flashlight, its beam casting another oval of light on the floor. He flicked it up. *"Madre de Dios.* Trudie! What are you doing here?"

Trudie rubbed her eyes. "I don't know. I was going to test myself by trying to spend a night here. Then I heard you playing music in the back, and Susan and Nathan talking in the front hall, so I thought maybe something was scheduled to happen tonight. Is something scheduled? Do you want me to leave? Not that I'm going to."

"Susan?" said Julio.

"I had an idea. I didn't expect so much company." She spoke bitterly, on fire with unfamiliar anger.

"Don't get mad," said Julio. "Whatever happens, we have to live with ourselves. I have to do everything I can to stop you. If I didn't even try, that would drive me crazy."

"But you can't stop me." Susan felt the power she could wield in this house. She could pass over a threshold and bar them from following her. She could summon furniture for them to trip over in the dark. She could seal herself in the crawl space, although she was not sure she could afford the luxury of a leisurely death if they all knew her intentions. She would have to cut someplace closer to her heart than her wrists. "Besides, you won't have to feel guilty," she told Julio. "You can come see me here anytime. I'm sure House won't mind."

"There's no guarantee you'll end up here," Julio said. "You can't dictate to Death—can you? Can she, Nathan?"

"I couldn't. Listen, Susan: You'll lose your senses,
except for sight and sound, every day of the year except
one. You'll lose your freedom and all sense of purpose.
No growth, no aging, no increase of any kind, nothing to
look forward to except once-a-year freedom. Other times
of the year, you can't even smell the sea. And this is only
if you *do* end up here. The further journey is still that
undiscovered country, as far as I'm concerned. The best
thing that's happened to me in fifteen years is your coming here, and we can't expect another you to come along
fifteen years from now."

"But don't you see? It's all changed. Our friends
come, and when they grow up, they can send their children. Like Peter Pan, and this house our Neverland. We
can become—an institution." She felt lit up with grin,
like a Halloween pumpkin.

"You're contemplating suicide?" Trudie asked clini-
cally.

Susan nodded.

"Why? What is it you can't talk about? Tell me
something concrete this time, instead of abstract.
What's really wrong?"

Susan clutched her elbows, hunched her shoulders.
With the armor gone, the words she had found impos-
sible to say came out. "Go to my house and ask my
mother," she said. Her teeth knocked together. "Go to
my house and ask my mother, if she can get up to answer
the door."

Shivering started, and knotting in her stomach. She

felt an upwelling of misery such as she had never known, wave after wave sweeping through her, but this time the pain had a name. She couldn't escape into it. She was guilty, guilty of causing terrible suffering, she didn't deserve happiness, she didn't even deserve to live. She had had one chance after another to behave correctly, and she had always failed. She was flawed, no matter what Father said, and the only way she could end her mother's suffering was by killing herself. She didn't care what became of her ghost.

She pulled herself together enough to dash between them and run upstairs, slammed the door to her room behind her. She crept into the crawl space, heard the panel shut behind her, and huddled beside Nathan's bones, in darkness. In darkness she took his thumb bone out of her pocket and set it gently with the others. In darkness, she took out the knife.

"No," Nathan said. His hands closed over hers.

"You can't touch me," she whispered. She had set the thumb bone down, and she wasn't touching the others.

He slid the wrapped knife out of her hands. It was as if it vanished; without his bone, her house sense fogged so that she could read only general information. "How can you touch me?"

"I don't know. Something's happening in House. Edmund and Deirdre are doing things in the attic. Or maybe it's because you're so close to my bones." He touched her cheek.

She pressed her hand over his cool hand on her cheek, trapped his touch.

"Your dream is so comfortable," he said. "I almost wish it could come true, but I don't think there's hope of that. It was a mistake when I did it, and it would be a mistake for you to do it. Don't give up on blood and breathing yet. There's so much you can do with your life, and there are consequences to suicide you can't even guess at."

"Who makes the rules?"

"It's complicated," he said. She put her free hand up to his face, touched his smile.

"You don't know what will happen, any more than I do." She knew he felt her cheek shift as she smiled into the darkness. "Give me back my paring knife."

"Paring knife?"

"Father doesn't use razor blades."

"Perhaps you should wait until we can install a guillotine."

"Maybe I could buy some rope. That would be more romantic. We could be a matched set."

"That's ghoulish." He slipped his hand from under hers, and gripped her hands. "Susan."

She sighed. He wouldn't give her back her knife; she knew that. Her plan would have to wait. Maybe it would be better if she did it at home, anyway. That way Father would know he had no reason to hurt Mother anymore.

Why hadn't she thought of that before? Killing

herself wasn't going to save Mother, not if Father didn't even know what Susan had done. He would only know she was gone, and when Susan was gone, Mother—

"I have to go home!" If she went home and slipped back inside without anyone knowing she had been gone—maybe she *could* be perfect. Maybe just long enough to figure out a new and better plan.

All she had to do was stop wanting anything.

"Wait," whispered Nathan. "Something's happening. Wait. I have to go." He released her hands. She reached blindly out in the darkness. Her fingers found the bones that had once caged his heart. Her house sense opened wide.

The others had all gone up to the attic. Five knots of energy shimmered around a circle that flamed on the floor. Deirdre, Edmund, Julio, Trudie, and Nathan.

There was a strange synchronization about them. She remembered where she had felt it before: Julio's energy felt like that when he played the violin. She heard the notes of the mandolin faintly through the walls.

In the center of the circle was a small dark knot, dense with energy. She focused on it, touched it with her house sense. Suddenly she was in the midst of her own memories of her day by the sea. Her sea stone: Edmund must have taken it from the stove.

The air in the attic was thick with power. Julio's

music helped focus it. Edmund spoke words that shaped it. The energy swirled around the circle, each person adding to it as it passed, more coming from the floor they sat on, House adding energy of its own.

And then the spiral of energy came to her.

She felt tingling electricity as power flowed into her like water into a cup.

What were they doing to her? How had Edmund directed this at her? What was she supposed to do with it?

She wanted to send all this power home to Father. If only she could strike Father, beat him down. Hot red rage rocketed through her, unknown and terrifying; she imagined her father whimpering and trying to crawl away from her while she beat him. She imagined that he had no escape.

Her stomach tightened even more, until she felt like she would throw up. No. Her friends had given her this power. If she used it to turn into the kind of person her father was—

She thought of her mother, of bone-deep bruises, all the things that hurt, all the things that her mother would have to live with, to hide. Today's beating was probably the worst one yet; Susan had done more to earn it than ever before. Gone when her father expected her to be home. Dirty when she came home late, and with Julio, someone her father had forbidden her to see.

*Oh, Mother. I'm sorry. I should never have started sneaking out.*

197

The power surged in her, waiting for her to choose a direction and send it out to do work.

Susan's mind sought her mother. *Can this be comfort? Can this be healing?*

She felt her mother's sleeping presence, the deep and shallow pains all through her. The power, warmth, and comfort flowed from Susan into her mother, poured into the broken places, and washed away the hurt. Strength and healing, the best gift she had ever had to give her mother, passed through Susan and went home. The power felt tender and strange as it left her, sweet and sharp as an aftertaste of mint.

Her mother woke, shifted, sat up. "What?" she whispered. She touched her cheek, a kiss of fingers, not a probing of a wound. A soft, wondering "Oh."

Susan lost her connection then. Drained, she leaned against the crawl space wall.

*They gave me a gift. I made it into another gift and gave it away.*

She hadn't turned into her father.

She had helped her mother.

But what would happen next time her father got angry?

Maybe she could live so there wouldn't be a next time. Do everything Father said, meet all his expectations. Abandon herself and live Shadow's life.

But she had been trying to do that for years, and it hadn't worked so far.

She remembered showing Trudie the blood in her

palm. What had she locked up inside herself? Tonight she had felt her own fury and rage. She couldn't pretend anymore that she had no feelings. Somehow her feelings would creep out of her, and then someone would get hurt, the way Mother got hurt when Father's feelings came out.

She couldn't count on people handing her magic when she needed it again.

Could she?

Knocks sounded on the secret panel. "Hey. You alive in there?" asked Deirdre's voice.

Susan sighed and sagged against the wall. She took a few deep breaths. She had to go out there. She wouldn't mind falling asleep right here. Or just sitting here until she died.

That would waste everything. The healing, the chance to show her father what she was going to do so he would leave Mother alone. She pulled herself together and crept out to face her friends.

Edmund held the Coleman lantern, its cool, blue-green light spilling over them all. "You okay?"

"Tired," she said. "What did you do?"

"We tried a spell. It was the only thing I could think of."

Julio said, "No way we could get to you if the house didn't want us to, except by sending something that can go through walls. Did it work?"

"It worked enough to stop you from killing yourself," Deirdre said. "Right?"

"Yes. I took your magic and gave it to Mother so she wouldn't hurt anymore." She stared at the floor for a long moment. "I better go home. I'm sorry I caused everybody so much trouble. Thank you for the magic. That helped a lot. Thank you for caring what happens to me."

"What changed?" Trudie asked. "This whatever it was we did that I don't understand or believe in, it stopped you, right? But the reasons for suicide are still there. Or did the magic make them go away?"

Susan shook her head. "I couldn't figure out what to do with the magic so the reasons would go. Maybe if I were smarter—" She shook her head. "Maybe there's something I could do. I'll have to think about it. Right now I have to go home."

"Wait a sec. All that work and it didn't solve the problem?" Deirdre said. "You're still thinking—?" Deirdre pulled a pencil and a tiny notebook out of her raincoat pocket, scribbled something on a page, and tore it out to hand to Susan. "Before you do anything final, promise you'll call me. Let me talk you out of it."

Susan took the piece of paper and tucked it into her jacket pocket. "I can't."

"Susan," Julio said.

"I won't make a promise I can't keep," she said. "I have to go." She couldn't imagine that anything good would come out of her going home now, but it would be worse if she didn't go. "Excuse me." She pushed past them on her way to the door.

The door slammed shut before she could go through it.

She grasped the doorknob, turned it, tugged. The door refused to open.

Now she knew how the others felt when House wouldn't respond to them. Angry, frustrated, afraid.

She leaned against a wall, pressed her palms flat, sought her sense of House. *Won't you talk to me?*

*Always and forever,* House murmured.

*I have to leave, House.*

*First you have to promise Deirdre. Promise Julio. Promise Edmund, Nathan, Trudie, and me. Promise us you won't take your own life.*

*Don't you want me?*

*Always and forever,* whispered House, *but you don't have to be dead. I have you already.*

Susan felt weariness in her bones.

"What is it?" Edmund asked.

"I have to promise I won't kill myself, or House won't let me leave."

No one said anything. They watched her.

She rattled the doorknob some more. Heat lodged in a lump in her throat. When would people ever stop telling her what to do? She lowered her head and let her hair fall over her face.

"All right," she said to the floor. "I promise that I won't make another attempt without trying to contact someone about it."

"That's not good enough," Trudie said.

"What do you mean?" Susan tilted her head back, let

her hair part so she could stare at the other girl.

"Trying isn't enough. You have to actually talk to somebody, and give them a chance to talk you out of it."

Susan shook her head. "All right," she said. "I promise."

A moment went by when nothing changed. What did she have to do to get home? Would she get to stay here forever after all?

The knob turned in her hand, and the door creaked open.

"I'll walk you home," Julio said.

"We all will," said Edmund.

Susan glanced at Nathan, who stared back at her, his face serious. She went to the secret panel and crept into the crawl space. *You know the one I want,* she thought, and put her hand down where Nathan's skeleton waited. A bone moved under her fingers. She picked it up. The thumb metacarpal. Her hand closed around it, and she felt a strange peace, comforted by the familiar, her thing of power.

She crawled out into the room. "All right. I'm ready now."

They left the house together, all six of them. She didn't know how far Nathan could come with them; since she held the bone, he could at least come outside.

As Susan walked through the night, surrounded by friends, strange things happened inside her.

Nothing good waited at the end of this journey, but right now, she was with people who asked for hard promises because they cared about her future.

The sense of belonging, of leading a normal life that she had had for that brief moment in the school locker room when the other girls teased her about her boyfriend, that was a taste of what she had always longed for. Now she had people who knew some of her secrets, people who had shared their own. No normal lives here, but shared lives.

Nathan's cold hand slipped into hers. She meshed her fingers with his.

She couldn't imagine a good future, but in this moment, she felt strangely contented. Maybe she could live through tomorrow, if she could just remember that no matter what happened at home, she had someplace else to go, other people to see. She glanced at Trudie in the orange streetlight, saw half a smile. Deirdre wore her purple slicker and a scowl. Julio and Edmund looked grim. They all walked clumped around her. She almost felt safe.

They walked in silence to Shannon Hill.

"Maybe I can still make it inside without Father knowing I was gone," Susan said. "From here on, I need to sneak."

"We'll be quiet," said Julio.

Nothing could silence Deirdre's tendency to stomp, but Father wasn't a great listener to things outside of the house.

The closer they got to home, the more uneasy Susan felt.

Light shone out through the long thin slits of window in the living room.

"Something happened," Susan whispered to her friends. "He's waiting up."

They edged up the street out of sight of the living room windows.

"Is he looking out? What's he doing in there?" Susan murmured.

"I've made it this far." Nathan looked up toward the house. "I'll go scout." He vanished.

In silence Susan watched mist pearl around streetlights in the town below. Cars carried people from one place to another, maybe to warm places. In the distance, the ocean slid up the sand and retreated, returned, retreated, *hush hush hush.*

A moment later Nathan rejoined them. "He's sitting in the living room reading a newspaper. There are pieces of the paper all over the floor. He looks worried and confused."

"He made a mess? In the living room? That's so unlike Father. . . . The living room." Susan pressed her fist against her chin. Would he hear her if she sneaked in through the kitchen door? The well-oiled kitchen door, several rooms away from the living room. But how could she climb the stairs? The living room was only a door away from the stairs, and Father was always too aware of her movements inside the house, as though he had a house sense of his own. "If only I can sneak up to my room and change and get into bed without him knowing."

"We could distract him," Trudie whispered.

"How?"

"Make strange noises or ring the doorbell or something."

"Ringing the doorbell won't help, because the front door's right by the stairs. The stairs are the tricky part."

"If we made noise out here, would he look out the window first?" Trudie asked.

"Yes. He likes looking out those windows."

"Nathan, can you go with Susan and tell us when she needs a distraction?" said Julio.

"Of course."

Susan and Nathan crept around the house to the kitchen door. He went through the wall, then came back and nodded. She slipped out of her shoes and sneaked into the house.

They went to the kitchen door. Nathan vanished. Two minutes later he returned. "He's still reading the paper. He picks up sections, looks at them, shakes his head, and drops them again," he murmured.

"I don't understand that. He's always sure of himself."

"Well." Nathan shrugged.

"If they can distract him now, I'll run upstairs."

Nathan nodded and disappeared.

A moment later, Susan heard strange howls outside the house. "Now," Nathan said beside her. "He's looking out."

She ran for the stairs, fear pounding beside her. She stepped around the noisy spots on the steps and dashed into her room, closed the door silently.

Susan took off her dirty clothes, rushed into her bathroom and brushed her hair, washed her hands and face, gave her teeth a quick scrub. She glanced at her fingernails. Dirty! She used a fingernail brush to get them clean. Father always checked her fingernails.

She hid the dirty clothes in the back of her closet, behind all the clean clothes. For good measure, she took the dirty clothes from her earlier expedition to the haunted house that afternoon out of her laundry hamper and hid them in the closet, too, then straightened everything so it looked undisturbed. She put on a pink flannel nightgown, crept into bed, and turned off the bed-table light.

Chill came to her in the dim room. "He went outside to see what was making the noise, but everybody hid in time. Now he's coming upstairs," Nathan whispered.

Susan touched her hair. Yes, she had brushed it. She hid Nathan's bone under her pillows, then snuggled against the pillows and pulled the covers up to her chin. She slowed her breathing to sleep rhythm and let her eyes fall shut.

Such a long, exhausting day. She was ending it at home. Not what she had planned.

A door opened in the house: the door to her mother's room. Footsteps of her father walking around her mother's bed. No sound from her mother.

Her mother, who would no longer be marked from the earlier beating if Susan had used her friends' magic the way she thought she had. No wonder Father was confused. Brand Mother with bruises and, a couple hours later, find the marks gone? How could Father possibly understand that?

Breathe slowly.

The door shut. Footsteps in the hall. Her bedroom door eased open. The overhead light switched on, an unpleasant glare.

"Princess?" said Father, his voice hoarse.

Susan blinked like a sleeper waking. She glanced about—no Nathan in sight, though she felt his cool presence. "Father?"

"Where have you been?"

Her hands clenched into fists under the covers. "Here," she said.

"No. You were gone earlier tonight."

"I did my homework after supper and went to bed, Father."

"You were gone."

To deny any statement he made was a mistake. Susan kept silent.

"Weren't you gone?"

"I went to school today," she said.

"Weren't you gone tonight?"

"Where would I go?" she whispered.

He stared at her. He paced through her room, flipped open the schoolbooks on the desk, looked at her homework assignments. Then he disappeared into the bathroom. She heard the laundry hamper open and close, imagined him touching her towels and toothbrush to see if she had used them. Of course they would be damp. They were every night when she had prepared for bed.

He came back out. "Let me see your hands and feet."

Her feet! She hadn't washed her feet.

She held out her hands, and he inspected her fingernails, her palms. Then he stripped back the covers and lifted her nightgown to look at her feet.

She had worn shoes all day, except for those moments when she sneaked around wearing only socks. Was that enough? She lay unmoving while he studied the soles of her feet. He pulled the covers back up over her and tucked them in tight, imprisoning her in the bed.

"Sleep well." He went to the door. He turned out the light, still watching her.

She breathed.

Gently, he shut the door.

Inside her, a strange heat blossomed.

Father was confused, uncertain. She had never seen him like that before.

Magic.

She had had life-and-death adventures, and he didn't

know anything about them. She had helped her mother in a way he would never understand. Maybe, with help, she could do it again.

Help. She had help: here in the room with her, and outside, ready to howl as necessary, or send her power. She had friends now, friends who thought of new answers to problems when she couldn't.

Her father might hold her shadow, but he couldn't cage her heart.

He didn't own her friends. He didn't even own a piece of Julio, the only one whose name he knew. Today he had fired Juanita, but he would rehire her. He had done it before. Juanita was the only one in town who would work for him, and he was addicted to a spotless house. Juanita would be back: another friend.

What about Susan's own house? Nathan's house said it would accept her whenever she came, but Susan had to live in this house, the house her father had designed. Susan's house had its dark sides, its cache of horrible secrets; it also offered her secrecy, safety, shelter, and the knowledge of what other people inside it were doing.

She reached past her headboard to place her palm against the wall. *House?*

Mother slept in her room, her breathing easy. Father paced in his study, still agitated. The house told her these things more clearly than she'd ever sensed them before.

*House?*

After a long wait, a deep, sleepy voice answered her. *Smallest?*

*House.*

The house didn't reply again, but it had answered once.

She could wake it.

Time to work on her second experiment.

If she could wake her own house, maybe she could get it to help her.

Maybe Nathan could help her wake the house. She reached under the pillows, closed her hand around the bone. Her special sense widened.

Nathan had left.

She let go of the bone.

Alone again.

Then a breath of refrigerated air came to her. "Maybe, if your father thinks things never happened, or can't figure out what *did* happen, he won't do anything."

"Yes," she whispered. "Let Father doubt."

"Now that you're safely back, do you still need the others outside?"

For a moment she didn't answer. She savored the thought of friends waiting to protect her from her father. Individually, none of them could stand up to him, but together, maybe they could manage.

Together.

"They can go," she said at last. "Please tell them thanks, thanks a million times."

She gripped the bone, and felt Nathan blow out like a flame. She sighed and slowed her breathing again.

Before she drifted into deep sleep, she felt Nathan's presence return to the room.

"Sleep," he whispered. "I'll watch."

She slept.

**Nina Kiriki Hoffman** is the author of six acclaimed novels, including two sequels to this one– *A Red Heart of Memories*, which was a finalist for the World Fantasy Award, and *Past the Size of Dreaming*. She has also written and sold more than two hundred short stories, which have appeared in anthologies and magazines.

Her short stories and novels have been finalists for the Nebula, the World Fantasy, and the Endeavor Awards. Her book *The Thread That Binds the Bones* won the Bram Stoker Award for first novel, and her short story "A Step into Darkness" won a Writers of the Future Award back in 1984.

Nina lives in Eugene, Oregon, with cats, friends, and many creepy toys.